I0547391

A Future Imperfect

A Novel

Kosonike Koso-Thomas

Sierra Leonean Writers Series

A Future Imperfect

Copyright © 2017 by Kosonike Koso-
Thomas All rights reserved.

No part of this book may be reproduced in any
form by paper, electronic, or other means
without the written permission of both
the author and the publisher

*This is a work of fiction. Except in a few obvious instances, names,
places, institutions and incidents are either products of the author's
imagination or have been used fictitiously. Any resemblance to actual
events, places, or persons alive or dead is purely coincidental*

ISBN: 978-9988-8698-3-0

Sierra Leonean Writers Series

Part I
The Final Straw

Chapter 1

The paved road that goes up the 1,000-foot mountain range of the Matapata Hills is one of the steepest in the town of Manola. The narrow four-kilometre stretch of road snakes its way along the bottom, bypassing the residential areas and the sprawling slums around them and climbs up hill to the town's only university. It is a picturesque route that offers breathtaking views. Set apart from the hustle and bustle of the town in the valley, few pedestrians used this steep mountain road to reach the gates of the university campus at the top. Students were always bussed in or arrive by private or public vehicles from the town's central bus station and lorry park in the commercial district. The university itself is perched on the lower ranges of Matapata, across which, it extended to cover an area of two hundred and fifty square kilometres of rolling land. From the campus, the Saluka resort, with its white sandy beach and its eighteen-hole golf course, presented a stunning distant view.

To be a student living in such a natural environment was a privilege, not often appreciated. Particularly by students admitted after the national government instituted free university education, two decades ago. A presidential order had revoked the university's private status and taken responsibility for meeting all costs.

This was a unique campus, in a country whose history is linked with the ancient empire of Songhai, also known as

Songa in the language of the indigenous people. It was rarely called by its colonial name. Other countries have done likewise, who have felt it a service to the dignity of former African empires. Songhai, the empire, once stretched across a vast territory, most or which has been partitioned into smaller modern states, some facing the Atlantic Ocean.

The college campus in Manola was designed as a garden city, where learning centres and domestic accommodation blended into the surrounding hills of that part of the country. The Grounds and Gardens Department had created flower displays in a tropical assortment. There were orchids in full bloom dancing side by side with sweetly- scented lilies. Red and white rose bushes arranged in cloisters, relieved the sparseness of the stray flowers sticking out delicately from the deep red soil that anchors their roots. Every hundred metres the beds widen into mini gardens. Arranged in the middle of each of these was a circular paved area on which sturdy metal chairs sit artfully in a semi-circle.

Inspector Borah, the university's chief security officer, and his staff had just completed their early morning patrol when they detected a crowd assembling at the gates of the university. Some of them looking intimidating, which caused them concern. Inspector Borah rushed to open the gates. The angry crowd surged past him into the main university driveway, which five years earlier, was named University Way. The inspector realised that he was facing a crisis that his limited force may find hard to handle. There had been student demonstrations on this campus before, but he had experienced no disturbance in the two years since his appointment. Stunned by the force of the protest, he summoned up all his authority as he barked "Disperse immediately!" to the crowd. "We are peaceful students demanding permission to hold a peaceful demonstration," a tall athletic male said as he stepped forward with a bank of paper under his arm. He presented a single note to the inspector. Borah retreated from the crowd to read it. He moved back and said, "From what I can judge, you are not inclined to holding a peaceful demonstration. Under university laws, you are not permitted to disturb the peace of this campus."

Across from him on one side of the crowd, someone shouted, "Get out of the way, or you will be sorry!" Borah's mood changed. He shouted back, "You are the ones who will be sorry if you don't disperse," he warned. Suddenly, students from the rear of the crowd rushed, forcing those in front to push past Borah, almost bringing him to the ground. They then started marching down the driveway, chanting and drumming on tin sheets and empty oil drums. Borah picked himself up and made for the security post to warn the administration of the danger.

Sounds from the demonstration echoed across the buildings that lined both sides of University Way. Male and female voices melded into a discord that floated with the wind across the campus. The peace and order once again threatened by disruption at a time when lectures were about to start after the first semester break. The front line of marchers were holding banners accusing the university administration of various failures, such as the deterioration in academic standards and the shabby student halls on campus. Many were carrying placards demanding that the Vice Chancellor should be replaced, because they saw him as ineffective in making improvements that were vital to restoring the university to its old glory.

The motley crew of marchers fanned out across the road into the well-tendered flowers, crushing them with their shoes and boots; disregarding notices warning people to keep off lawns and flower beds. When the crowd heaved past the university's guest house, groups of male students started breaking from the line. They smashed doors and window panes on buildings on both sides of the road and barked threats at anyone who dared to stop them. For over a century, the best leaders of thought in this country were educated there. This was a university whose stature was acknowledged, not because of its contribution to the mainstream of world scientific and technological knowledge, but because it had been there at the earliest awakening of human intellect in this region of the world. Its attraction within and outside the country had not waned and many chose to come there because their fathers and grandfathers had. Unfortunately, students' unrest had been more regular recently. It is believed that the trend was a direct result of the establishment of youth wings of political parties at the university campus. The university authorities have been unable to deal with this impact of politics on campus life.

In the middle of the crowd were girls from Brend Hall. They had agreed to join the march after the Student's

Union President assured them that the march would be peaceful. He told them that it would be a quiet procession from the University Bookshop to the administrative quadrangle, with students displaying placards. The march would end in front of the VC's office, where he would deliver a petition, demanding improvements to students' facilities. Jennoh, one of the Brend Hall girls, disturbed by the boisterousness and vandalism into which the march had descended, turned to her hall colleagues protesting. "This is not what we bargained for," she said. Dorma, one of her closest friends was walking behind her and sensed her regret in taking part.

"We should have known that Sidney Titmus could not control the mob around him," she remarked.

"I agree. He was very convincing and we fell for the Titmus charm."

"Titmus is only a figurehead," Dorma commented. "Those radical boys around him are the ones who really run the union. He was chosen, because they knew he had the charisma and a silver tongue to win votes, particularly the female votes."

"As for me, Jennoh, as soon as we reach the quadrangle, I am backing out.

"Why go that far? We should leave now before violence breaks out," Jennoh said. She pulled Dorma out of the line and stood with her on the side of the road for a while. More of the girls from the crowd joined them, as they walked away in the opposite direction, back to Brend Hall.

They passed the gate leading to the university sports field, then turned right into Kanto Road.

Chapter 2

Mudu Kolen was walking from his office in the Arts building to the Rema Lecture Theatre for his first lecture of the day when he heard the noise of the marching crowd. To reach the lecture theatre from Lomba Street, he had to walk along University Way and take the turning into the University's Conference Centre, where the lecture theatre was located. The conference centre was an impressive state-of-the-art complex, which also housed the University's House of Prayer. He was expected to give his first lecture at 8.30 a.m. It was a dull February morning. The dry cold north-westerly winds bearing fine dust, had blocked much of the sun's rays. Kolen hated this season, which could last for another month. Apart from covering his study desk and kitchen utensils, the yellow dust went up to his nostrils and stifled his breathing.

This annual attack frustrated him. He had been given medication to clear the allergy, but there were days when he felt it did little to relieve his suffering. That morning, he was glad that the medication worked. He was breathing in the cold air with its air -borne menace that left his nasal passage unaffected. He felt no concern about his safety as he moved on, crossing Freshers Lane. The riotous racket did not bother him. He felt that he was an unlikely target of any student demonstration. He was a senior lecturer of three year's standing, yet had neither an administrative role in his department nor one in the wider university structure. He turned right at the next junction into Tomo Street and walked briskly till he

8

reached the junction of University Way. He stood on the side of the road intending to watch the crowd pass, after which he could move on to his lecture.

As the crowd drew nearer, the roar became deafening. Shouts of, "Malu must go," rose from the leaders in the front row. To Kolen, the sound seemed to ricochet, returning in a spherical wave, as if reflected from an invisible plane surface. The clash of sound was yielding discordant noises. The crowd seemed determined to wreck the campus, caring little about the consequences. Kolen was viewing the scene from a closer distance now.

In the staff club, there were lecturers seated around tables in the lounge, chatting near the coffee bar. Some had late morning lectures, others had no lectures for the day. The club was a popular staff meeting and relaxation centre. It was an elegant club. Large glass windows dominate the east and west walls of the building. Curtains hung from wooden rods slotted into steel brackets, their pale blue and orange fabric stamped with abstract images looked graceful, an inch or so above the club's timber floor. You entered the club through a door on its southern side, but once you are in, the recess into which the door was fitted became undetectable, its form merging into the rest of the wall artfully covered in a boarded finish. The complement of wood and brightly painted drapes give off an aura of gaiety, as if intended to dispel any despondency in those struggling to cope with the pressures of aggressive academic competition. In addition to two lounges with settees and arm chairs, the club had a dining room, a games room and a small reading room; its walls lined with bookshelves. The lounge had coffee and wine bars. Photographs of presidents of past academic staff associations hung neatly on the walls. Dr. Manda was at the counter speaking to Dr. Salleh, each nursing a cup of coffee. They were discussing the outcome of the legal battle between the Manola Timber Industries and the government over the company's violation of the terms of their logging agreement. The Manola town council had been complaining to the government for years about the illegal extension of the limits of concession without action being taken to call the industry to account. Now action had been taken but the settlement had been disputed by the council as it did not receive adequate compensation for the loss of revenue for unrecorded tonnes of logs shipped from logging sites.

Manda believed that the court's award of compensation could be challenged in an appeal's court, but there were other issues to deal with. His father lives in the town and he should know.
"The main issue has still not been resolved," he said. "It is not the level of compensation awarded by the court that matters to the   people, it is the unfairness of partitioning of the royalty paid by the industry that is their concern. The community believes that the forest is theirs and that they should be the major beneficiary of any royalty arrangement with government," Manda said.
Saleh listened attentively. He put his hand over the rim of his cup and spoke. "I can understand that. But will the government understand it? Every one of the politicians who come from this area dash off to the city after their election. It is the local people who bear the

10

brunt of the impact of logging on their environment and their livelihood. The community is gradually losing forest from which so many ordinary people depend," he said.

"I know that an association has now been established with the clear title of Manola Forest Protection Association (MFPA). My father hopes that the association will be the best lobby for their cause. The irresponsible degradation of the environment should stop." Manda spoke without conviction, knowing that maintaining an association of that nature, operating so far from the seat of power, could be a challenge.

He was about to order some more coffee when one of the club attendants ran in to warn that students were holding a demonstration on campus. Their discussion quickly turned from logging violations to students' protests.

"I am shocked that another students' demonstration is taking place so soon after the last one six months ago," Manda volunteered a comment.

That incident was captured by the national press. Then, the university was able to settle the disturbance through the intervention of the Ministry of Education. Apparently, the settlement was not far-reaching, because it stopped short of reviewing the university's financial and administrative structures, which the students had called for. It was widely known that most of the academic staff also believed that there ought to be proper reviews of these structures as, according to them, they were not working properly. The Triennial Grants Commission that was set up by government to review the university's proposals for funding all activities over a three-year period had made recommendations, which had not been implemented in full. That was causing disaffection among staff and students on the campus.

"Government has to meet its obligations to higher education, and do that quickly before the system crumbles further," Salleh said.

"With the present state of the country's economy, government has to trim budgets even of priority areas like security," Manda countered.

"But it is foolhardy to make university education free, so all students who qualify can enter university. If the government could not afford free university education, why did it have to introduce it?"

Manda was surprised that sentiments like those could come from one who had benefited from free education, since he entered secondary school to the end of his university education. It was known that in the years following the country's independence, there was a shortage of skilled manpower to fill vacancies left by departing colonial officers. That had affected the successful implementation of the country's development plans, particularly in sections of the mining, fishing, and agricultural industries. The free education policy was introduced to solve that problem and had increased the supply of qualified administrators and technical staff to man those key areas of the country's economy. Manda reminded him of this.

"Well, this is the platform on which the last government fought and won the election," he said. "It had to go through with it, continuing the policy favoured by all political parties since independence."

Manda had heard much of Salleh's sentiments before. They were shared by other colleagues. Many have complained about poor staff conditions and the delay in improving them. The last set of negotiations with the university court to revise staff conditions took place four years ago. They often point to a deterioration in facilities in the academic and administrative departments and in staff and students' accommodation. Academics everywhere are always sensitive about conditions which may impact on the quality of their work, and they can be quite passionate when expressing their disaffection with their employers.

Salleh dismissed Manda's argument. "It is not a question of money alone; it is management deficit."
Manda sensed some spite in his voice. He felt he was stepping into a boxing ring with an opponent expecting him to fight for the Vice Chancellor's corner. He accepted the invitation.
"The way everything is blamed on the VC makes him feel as if a chain of wrought iron had been hung around his neck."
"Maybe so, because he doesn't have a clue about managing people," Salleh countered. "What you forget is that without increased funding from government, the Vice Chancellor can do very little to satisfy all staff and students' demands."
"Look, Manda, when he knows the government cannot provide all the funds the university needs, why has he

not devised plans to generate funds from within and outside the university? Malu lacks the skill to raise funds for the university. The job of a Vice Chancellor is to build on the foundations he inherits. He cannot afford to preside over the retrogression of what others have built."

Both Manda and Salleh had begun to raise their voices to a pitch that other members could hear. Soon a number of them moved over to join them. Salleh now had an audience to play to. He seemed to relish the opportunity. He moved from his seat at the bar and stood to give his assessment of the conditions that he thought had given rise to recent students' riots. Manda listened uncomfortably as Salleh turned his rhetoric to the evaluation of the performances of past Vice Chancellors. It sounded like a prepared speech. Dipping his hands into his pockets, he said:
"Colleagues, we all know what the former Vice Chancellor did for this university during his 10-year stint here Although he had the ear of government because of his warm and genial personality, he did not rely on government funding only. He wooed industry, including Manola Forest Industries, to fund research activities and pay for the construction of faculty buildings, student dormitories, and scientific equipment. In his time, well-wishers were encouraged to donate funds that he would use to execute his plans. He had the knack for bringing people together, to do things. We are yet to see his successors achieve that level of success. The elegant campus infrastructure most of us boast of today was planned and executed during his period as VC."

Some in the group around them cheered. It made Manda uncomfortable. He came off the stool and attempted to leave. Salleh called out to him, "Don't go, we must finish this." Pride got the better of him. He turned around to face Salleh. To the onlookers, it seemed as if the two were about to ratchet up their verbal sparring into a physical bout. "We all know that Malu's immediate predecessor believed in maintaining the *status quo t*hat resulted in stagnation," Salleh continued. "That's why he was quickly booted out to bring in Malu Koney. Now, he is presiding over the university's progressive decay."

Manda allowed the heat of Salleh's outbursts to cool, then said, "I don't quite agree. We are still Number 1 in the country. I don't see any decay. Academic departments are still turning out first class graduates."
"Credit for that has to be given to staff who have dedicated their lives to their work. Credit cannot go to Malu who discourages initiative. That man lives in a cage. He seems to be unable to reach out to the government. No one throws money at a bad business. He has to convince government that he can deliver good academic products to the nation, if he is given the money to run such an important national institution," Salleh submitted, in a harsh tone.
"What more conviction do you want from the VC? The University Court is convinced he is doing a good job. The court is his boss," Manda said calmly.
"I have my doubts that Court is convinced about his management. Some members can see how badly things

15

are going. Students talk about shortages of basic facilities in the halls and lecture rooms," Salleh retorted.

Two months earlier, there had been a series of articles in the campus newspaper, *The Manola Review*, written by a hall warden arguing that poor facilities were making it harder for hall wardens to maintain discipline in their halls. Manda knew that Salleh was exploiting those comments. No doubt, some members of the university court would have read about these developments, apart from learning from students what was going on in the campus. He avoided mentioning this, and said only, "Salleh, these students can never be satisfied. In some of their homes, they will be lucky to have a quarter of the comforts they enjoy here."

"Let me tell you," Salleh retorted. "Students come here expecting to enjoy decent living conditions while studying to obtain qualifications for their future careers. Like us, they need an environment that is intellectually stimulating. Any discerning member of this campus could have predicted a recurrence of student's disturbance. And mark this; things are bound to get worse." He was seemingly agitated.

Manda remembered that Salleh was a contentious character. He had shown this offensive side two weeks earlier at an Academic Staff Association's meeting. The meeting was called to discuss the dismissal of Dr. Lame, a staff member who had leaked examination results to students before they were confirmed by the examination's board. At that meeting, it was proposed that notice of strike action be issued to the administration in response to the dismissal of a member. Salleh had been the proponent of that motion, which was defeated by a narrow majority. The reaction of Salleh and his supporters to that defeat was so awful, that they had to be bundled out of the meeting.

Manda rose to Salleh's threats. "You have shown that you are one of those lecturers who instigate students to violence," he spat back.

"And you? A Malu supporter, like Kolen, who stabs his colleagues on the back, for favours from the VC. We know you, squash-court traitors!"

"Is that another veiled threat?" Asked Manda

Salleh ignored him and walked out of the club into the back, frowning and muttering invective.

No one in the club could ever have imagined that one of their colleagues would be a victim of that riotous day.

Chapter 3

Standing with his file of notes piled high on his left arm, Mudu Kolen began having doubts about his decision to walk to University Way in the heat of the commotion. Before he could beat a retreat, he heard the crowd shout "Malu's crony! Chase him out! He is Malu's spy." He turned around and ran, heading for his office. A small group of students broke off from the main demonstration and turned into Tomi Street. The rest of the demonstrators pressed on towards the Administration Quadrangle, singing "We shall overcome". Few knew that there had been a breakaway group pursuing a lecturer. The group of four students chased him down the street. Modu Kolen had kept his 1.9 m. high athletic figure in prime shape. He had an early lead. He ran past Tomodu Guest House, then tried to get into the adjacent building which housed the University Bookshop. The doors were closed. There was now only a gap of 200 metres between him and his pursuers. They were closing in on him fast, as he turned into Lomba Street. Kolen noticed an open door to the front garden of the house at the junction of Fresher's Lane and Lomba Street. He dashed through it into the back of the house.

He looked quickly around the yard for a place to hide. He was in the middle of a well -tendered lawn. On his left was a paved patio with a bamboo top and wicker chairs arranged around it. It was the owner's garden sit-out. At the rear of the property was a vegetable garden. He could see the neat rows of sweet potato shoots with their tender green leaves spread out like a fan to catch what little of the morning sunlight came through the dusty air. On his right were a young mango tree and four tall pawpaw trees, demarcating the boundary on that side of the property. A small shed stood in front of the fruit trees and was open. Within were firewood bundles, piled high to the ceiling. There was no way a man of his size could squeeze in. He was in the open and anyone could find him. He rushed back from the lawn and made for the rear door of the house praying that it was unlocked. Before he could reach it, two bulky male students grabbed him by the shoulder, pulled him towards them and delivered several hard blows to his head. He tried to fight back, throwing punches. They missed their target. He resorted to kicking. That caught them by surprise and they backed off, but they returned with a fury that alarmed him. One of them drew out a pocket knife and struck him in the arm, then drove it into his back. Two other students who were in the chase joined in. He felt more blows striking him with quick succession. They could have been directed to other parts of his body, but all he felt was the pain coming from his head. He now tasted blood. It was oozing from a cut in his head and running down his face to his lips. He wondered whether he was going to be mutilated at the hands of those he was hired to teach. He had prepared himself through hard studies at this very university and at institutions abroad, to give back the best of the knowledge he had acquired. "Were the students worth it now?" he wondered. "What had he done to deserve this?" He had been good to students generally and particularly those in his department. He had helped many overcome their subject difficulties and some had received financial help from him. "Were some of them in the crowd? How odd would that be? How could anyone have accused him of being a stooge of the Vice Chancellor? These thoughts and more raced through his mind. Perhaps they knew that he and the VC were good friends. They played squash together regularly. They may have discovered that he had often defended his policies in discussions at the staff club. He knew that there were deep divisions among members of different student clubs, between the staff and the administration, between students and the administration and between students and their lecturers. In this divided academic landscape, crises sometimes flared up unexpectedly to engulf the entire campus population of this storied institution. However, this kind of attack on a lecturer was unheard of.

Mudu Kolen was in great pain now. He started to scream. His attackers silenced him with a hard kick to his groin. That brought him face down to the ground. He began to feel less of his pain and slowly lost consciousness. He saw himself walking on the sands of his home village of Pasande, his father waving him good luck as he jumped into a fishing boat and paddled out into the sea. A while later, he drifted back into consciousness and heard someone saying, "You guys have overdone it." Another said, "That will teach him a lesson." He felt dazed, drawn into a darkness which cleared when he made an effort to breathe. He saw himself back in the same boat. It was the boat in which his fisherman father had taught him to fish. He saw himself paddling further into the sea, the waves gently rocking the boat until the image faded into nothingness.

Chapter 4

Professor William Lasin was in his study on the top floor of his two-storey residence, preparing to leave for the day's lecture when his brother Tukima rushed into his study. Lasin had been at Manola for twenty-five years and had risen to the position of Professor of Zoology and Dean of Basic Sciences. He was highly respected on campus, not least for his research into the primates of the Gomoh forest. His work had helped determine the populations of the various species that inhabit this forest, which was once identified as the site of a National Park.

"*Bada*," his brother said. That was the title of respect used in the language spoken in Masere, the village of their birth, to address an elder sibling. "I saw some students running to the back of our house chasing a man. They may be students from the demonstration taking place. You remember, you asked me to shut the front and back doors of the house when we first heard the noise?"

"Do you recognize anyone?" His brother asked. "No *Bada*. Now they are fighting in the garden. It seems serious. Someone is in agony crying for help."

The professor quickly left his study and ran down the stairs. Tukima followed him shouting "*Bada*, don't go there these students are dangerous."

"Then let's call the police," the professor replied. He moved to the telephone stand and called the police post.

"Inspector Borah, Police Post." A strong baritone voice came clearly on the line.

"Hello Officer, this is Professor Lasin. There is disturbance in my backyard. I fear students are fighting out there. It appears quite serious."

"Can you identify them?"

"No."

"Are they connected with the rioting going on?"

"I can't tell."

"Well, we have our men at present at the Administrative Quadrangle, trying to prevent students damaging the administrative building and harming staff there and in the vicinity. We are quite stretched right now, but we've called in a contingent of riot police from Manor to help us deal with the situation. They are on their way."

"That will be too late, officer; someone might get badly hurt before the contingent arrives. I can hear screams coming from the garden. It sounds like someone's being tortured."

"Professor, I am sorry. All we can do is to wait for the riot police to arrive and then we would relieve some of our men at the administrative building and get them to then deal with the disturbance at your house."

"This is ridiculous. Are you telling me that you can do no better than that?"

"Yes, sir! The manpower and resources provided for the force here are insufficient to safeguard life and property on a campus of this size."

William slammed the phone down, realising that help from the police was as distant as heaven was from earth.

"Come on Tukima, we have to deal with the situation ourselves."

He rushed to the back door, unlocked it and pushed it wide open. As he stepped out onto the metal grill covering the backyard drain, he saw the last of the students running away from the yard. He tried to chase after them but then his eyes fell on the motionless body of a man blocking his passage to the garden. He involuntarily stepped back into the house. Regaining his composure, he came out again and looked closer at the battered body. He could see the right side of the face and recognized the well-sculptured goatee now stained with blood, as belonging to Dr. Modu Kolen. He was well known on the campus for his distinguished beard, a mark of elegance that many of his colleagues admired and a few envied. He looked like a man who had unexpectedly crossed the path of a voracious beast. There was blood everywhere on his clothes which had been ripped apart. Deep cuts covered his back, head, and chest, and his hands were tied behind his back.

"Let's call the hospital to send an ambulance," Tukima said, shocked by the extent of Kolen's injuries. "We can't wait, Tukima. I'll back up the truck from the garage. You keep an eye on him," Lasin said. As they left for the hospital, Lasin heard the sound of wailing sirens. "This is typical," he thought. "Police always arrive after the havoc has been done." Tukima could not stand the sight of blood, so he moved away from the body. He had barely taken a few steps when he heard laboured groans from Kolen. He moved closer and was surprised to see that Kolen was breathing rather heavily now. "Hurry, Bada, he may still be alive," he shouted out to his brother, who edged the truck to the side of the body. With great difficulty, both men gently hauled Kolen into the back of the truck.

Chapter 5

The University Hospital was located at the junction of Bamah and Tomo Streets. It was staffed by two doctors, four nurses, eight ward attendants, a pharmacist and two messengers and four cleaners. Students call it a glorified Sick Bay because it lacked an operating theatre and an intensive care unit to deal with serious accidents and emergencies. University residents believed these facilities were necessary, in view of the remoteness of the campus from larger towns in the district with up-to-date health facilities. Although plans for installing full scale health facilities on the campus had been approved, funds had still not been secured from the government to implement them. The hospital, however, had consulting rooms for doctors, three general wards and three treatment rooms. There was a limited number of basic equipment for less challenging emergencies.

By the time Professor Lasin and Tukima, arrived at the hospital, Dr. Kolen had lost a lot of blood. Apart from the bruises on his back, head, and chest, there were deep lacerations on his leg. He had slipped into unconsciousness since arriving at the hospital. Staff Nurse Frandoh, a tall slender figure, with an over-starched flying cap, was in charge at the emergency desk. She told the ward attendants to take the patient directly to Treatment Room 2 and asked the duty nurse to take the history of the case, while she hurried to the duty doctor's office.

The corridor to the doctor's office was long and narrow. The late morning sun had penetrated the open spaces in the ventilation block wall that bordered the street, lighting up the otherwise dark passageway. An intricate pattern of circular shadows made an intriguing image on the interior wall opposite, relieving it, albeit temporarily, of its austere blank white regulation paint.

The door to the doctor's room was open, revealing a large mahogany desk behind which he was sitting, attending to files piled before him. Against the wall to the right of his desk was an examination couch, to the right of which was a wash hand basin. Above the couch was an open window a meter and a half wide. A bank of two steel filing cabinets and a cupboard were lined against the wall to the left of his desk. Frandor stood at the door and spoke in an agitated voice, but with urgency.

"Dr. Korboh, a man has just been brought in with serious injuries to his head and body. He seems to be in a bad state," the staff nurse said?

Rising from his desk, he walked quickly out of his office, the staff nurse leading him.

"Do we know how he received those injuries?"

"Right now, as I speak, the duty nurse is taking the case history from Professor Lasin who brought him in." They entered the treatment room together and viewed the patient on the examination couch. "We have cleaned him up a little," the duty nurse said, handing the doctor the notes she had made on the case. He read them quickly. 'Assaulted by students; serious lacerations, head injury, barely conscious,' he read on. When he finished, he returned the notes.

Meanwhile, the demonstration had reached the quadrangle where the administrative departments of the university were located. There was no one in any of the buildings. Advice had reached them from the police post at the main gate to the campus, that all the buildings in the quadrangle be vacated, as a student demonstration was heading for the quadrangle, with suspected violent intentions. Once in the quadrangle, some of the students went on the rampage. Some threw stones at windows, shattering them to pieces. Others stormed into offices, breaking filing cabinets and emptying their contents on the floor. One group moved to the outer door of the Vice Chancellor's suite, chanting "Malu must go!" Breaking down the VC's door, they climbed the spiral staircase that leads to the suite. At the top of the stairs, they found their entrance barred by a solid steel door. It had been installed there after the last riot, when a band of unruly students forced their way in, seized the then VC, Malu's immediate predecessor, and frogmarched him to the student's cafeteria. They then got him to watch them dump food prepared for the day on the pavement, saying it was not fit for human consumption. When Malu succeeded him four years ago, it was thought that coming new with experience of academic life in both a local and a foreign university, he would be able to bring about the change that was desperately needed among students. Unfortunately, the culture of violent protests remained deeply rooted in the psyche of a disturbingly undisciplined group of students.

Angry at the unyielding steel gate that led into the VC's office, they retreated, leaving indecent graffiti on the walls as they trailed down the staircase. They then moved to the Quadrangle to join the rest of the students, who had formed a ring around the Union President, who was speaking.

"Fellow comrades," he was saying. "We cannot continue to endure the strains of living under conditions which deter our scholastic and social development." Interrupted every few minutes by wild cheers, he criticized the conditions on campus, comparing them with the comforts   students enjoyed in the new universities of the north. "There is only one way to end this suffering and bring lasting change to this University, the oldest and only years ago, the most respected in all of Africa. Malu must go," he said. As he rattled on, the riot police from Manor was moving closer to the quadrangle, their sirens growing louder every minute. The president shouted defiantly, "We are ready for them. We shall stand our ground.   It is our right to demonstrate and we will defend it.   We shall not surrender!"

Fifty meters from the quadrangle, the police alighted from their trucks. At the sight of them, some students began to slip away from the crowd. "You are ordered to disperse immediately," the commander of the force bellowed over his hand-held loud speaker. There was shuffling and bumping of bodies against bodies as some students forced their way out. The bulk of the crowd held their ground. Some began erecting barricades at the entrance to the quadrangle, using desks and chairs from the offices they had ransacked. They were singing and swaying their placards in the air. One hurriedly painted slogan read, "We will not tolerate any police brutality!" Others read, "We condemn poor student meals! "We condemn restrictions on travel outside campus! "More buses for students." The placards and signs had various messages for the authorities, but in the hostile climate, only their fellow protesters saw them.

Realizing that the students were determined to occupy the quadrangle, the police moved in with their riot gear, pushing them away from their makeshift blockade. The students fought back. In the encounter, five were arrested. Reaction from the crowd was swift. From the rear of their formation, they hurled stones and bottles into the lines of the advancing police. The police tactically moved behind the barricades. They then regrouped and shot rounds of teargas into the crowd. In the commotion, students were pushed back against the flank of policemen. Some ran into their shields, half blinded by the tear gas. The police commander ordered his men to open a corridor to allow withdrawing students to pass through. When it was finally over, the neat quadrangle was a wretched sight. Rocks, broken glass, and dismembered furniture were strewn across what had been a well tendered lawn. In all, forty students were taken to the university hospital with injuries. In addition to the five arrested at the start of the police offensive, ten others were taken to the police post for questioning. They were later released. They would face a panel of the Disciplinary Committee of the University. At the request of Inspector Borah, that part of the riot police remained. He hoped that their presence would deter any further disturbances.

Some of the girls who stayed with the demonstration after Jennoh and others had left, returned to their hall exhausted and visibly shaken. They had bruises on their hands and legs. They looked dishevelled, standing listlessly in the lounge. When the warden of the hall saw them, she sent her assistant, Miss Rogat, to summon them to her office. "The warden has asked me to tell you that she would like to see you girls in her office." They followed her out of the lounge.

Jennoh and Dorma were back in the lounge of their hall of residence when the rest of the girls arrived. They were sitting at a table by the garden window at the furthermost end of the room, talking. They felt angry at being tricked into joining such an unruly mob.

"The President has to be careful in dealing with some of the students whom he gathers around him. Some of them are quite militant," Jennoh said.

"I believe that among them are those who escaped from fighting in the border areas and who have been admitted into the university on concessional terms. Only God knows how these will be weeded out of the student body," Dorma replied.

There were four other girls sitting on lounge chairs reading. There was a girl at the piano, playing and singing religious songs.

"This is like being in church at Singspiration time," Jennoh whispered to Dorma.

"It's Monica, our Lady Superior of Brend," Dorma said.

"Ah Ah! Don't insult the Catholics," Jennoh exclaimed, raising her right hand like a police officer giving the stop sign to oncoming traffic."

"Sorry, I didn't know you were a Catholic. Anyway, she has been going about getting students to become 'Born Again' Christians. She says that their baptism in church was not enough. They would have to be baptised again to be true Christians."

"Don't apologise. I am not a Catholic. But don't you mind these 'Born Again' people. There are so many things they preach that many of them don't always follow."

"You remember Sando, the girl who was the Christian Union president two years ago?"

"Yes, I remember her."

"She was in Block C, room 24, just opposite my room. Every Friday, there was singing and praying in the room till midnight. You could hear the shouts of 'Hallelujah!', 'Praise the Lord!', 'Come down now Lord, show your power', and many other calls for divine uplift, ringing through our corridor."

"You must be joking," Jennoh said, amidst laughter that was drawing attention to them.

"You can laugh, but it wasn't that funny to be kept awake all night. You will be surprised. Our warden was there with them. You know that she is very religious and highly principled, don't you?"

"Yes, I remember her speeches at formal hall dinners, and her warnings about deceitful boys who prey on girls and leave them pregnant with no intention of marrying them."

"I was told that she holds prayer meetings also for committed 'Born Again' students where they make pledges of abstinence from alcohol and sex."

"Thank God she has not drawn me into that net," Jennoh said smugly.

"Well," Dorma said, leaning forward to touch Jennoh's arm, as if to get her full attention. "I was telling you about Sando. "You remember she was here when we all went to the registrar's office to sign on for our various courses in the first term?"

"Yes," Jennoh said.

"She was seen around for a while in the hall. Then she wasn't. Now she is back."

"What do you make of that?"

"My dear, don't be dumb. Girls go away to have it done."

"All that 'Born Again' training and they get laid in the shadows."

"Jennoh, that is the way the great deceit works. They show the world purity and uprightness, but behind the facade, lies dark minds covered in sin.

At the hospital, Professor Lasin was sitting with his brother in the waiting area when a group of students arrived, some with visible injuries. One of the students recognized him. He went up to him, "Sir, I hope there is nothing wrong. "

"Are you asking me?"

"I'm sorry sir, I thought you were waiting for treatment."

"Sure, treatment of the lecturer some of your militant colleagues battered nearly to death," Lasin spoke with

32

anger. "You students feel you own the world and do not have to be answerable to anyone," he continued. "Why should demonstrations be violent and why do you students not use the channels we have at the University for airing your grievances?"

"None of us here knows anything about that attack sir. Anyway, we shall report it to the Student's Union president".

"Well, we are waiting here to know from the doctor if there is a chance that the lecturer will survive his injuries".

"I assure you sir; the union will find the culprits and discipline them."

"That's beyond your union's remit now. It is in the hands of the police. They have been here already and taken statements from Tukima and myself."

As he spoke, he saw Dr. Korbo making his way from the treatment room through the group of injured students. He walked straight to Professor Lasin and said, "Please come with me to my room, Sir."

"Tukima, I'll be back," he said to his brother and followed the doctor to his consulting room.

They walked side by side along the narrow corridor to the doctor's office, not a word spoken between them. To Professor Lasin, the walk seemed like the longest he had taken within a building. Bad news, they say, takes longer to circulate than good ones. Dr. Korbo opened his office door and let the professor in. He offered him the seat by the side of his desk as he walked round to sit behind it.

"Now professor," he said. "I understand that you were the one who brought Dr. Kolen in after he was attacked by students."

"Yes, Doctor. And for my sins, the attack took place in my backyard. All that I told the police when they interviewed me in the waiting room. I believe the officers have also spoken to you when they were taken to see the patient in the treatment room."

"Do you know who his next of kin is?" The doctor asked with a solemn face.

The question worried him. He braced himself for the worst as his mind flashed back to the scene at the back of his house.

"That should be answered by the Registrar, who keeps these details in the staff member's file," he said. "However," he continued, " I know that he has a wife, who was a Senior Staff Nurse at Selak Hospital, at Clendon City, but has emigrated to the United States of America. They now live separate lives, I believe. But doctor, can I know what Kolen's condition is? I need to report this to the Secretariat and his dean."

"I understand your concern Professor, but in medical cases like this, we are required to identify the next of kin before we discuss treatment following our examination, especially where surgery may be required. For that to take place the signature of the next of kin is mandatory."

"That may be so. I have taken a personal interest in this case since I saved Kolen on my doorsteps. No doubt, the university will be sent your report. They will rely on your judgement to treat this staff member's injuries immediately. If it becomes necessary to provide a next of kin for more intrusive treatment, that will be handled by the administration." Dr. Korbo, put on a smile that suppressed his impatience at listening to the professor as he spoke. Then he said,

"We are treating this patient already. I appreciate your interest and concern for your colleague, but we must keep the patient's condition confidential. We would normally release it only to family members. As a mark of respect for your position and for the effort you made to save his life, I can only say that Kolen is still experiencing loss of consciousness. He shows signs of weakness and has developed nausea. The lacerations on his leg and shoulder have been stitched and bandaged and he is resting comfortably. We will continue to monitor him over the next two days in case other symptoms develop."

"Thank you," Lasin said. "There are students waiting for your attention. I hope there are no other serious cases like Kolen's to turn up."

"I doubt that. If there were any, they would have by now. The nurses seem to be dealing satisfactorily with what we have on hand at the moment."

Professor Lasin left the hospital with his brother, hoping that the man he tried to save, would receive the treatment his injuries require.

On the advice of the police, Malu had rushed to his residence before the rioting students got to his office. He was driven in his official car by one of the university's trusted drivers, Edayo, whom he had hired from Munga, his hometown. When he got home, he asked his driver to wait. He went into the house, and told his wife, Cecala, that there was trouble brewing in the campus and that they had to leave.

"Darling," he said, "You must have heard the commotion on the campus this morning, I do not think it will be safe to stay a minute longer, if the information I have received from the police and from my closest colleagues, is to be believed." Cecala could not quite grasp what her husband was saying. He had been welcomed with elation from the staff and students, who knew of his high academic achievements. They had been happy to have him as head of the institution, the spark to rekindle the flame of glory that the college once enjoyed. She had seen changes in attitude among the staff in the last two years, but she had waved this away as jealousy.

"How bad is it?" Cecala asked, tears welling up in her eyes.

"The rioting may get worse, if it resumes after the riot police leave. Apparently, our campus police could not cope, so the Chief Security Officer advised us to vacate the offices in the Administrative Complex for our own safety. He says the rioters are wild and are calling for my removal from office. In this situation, darling, we will not risk our lives staying here. This is a remote site and we may be harmed before help arrives."

"Where do we go?" She moved closer to her husband and hugged him, crying profusely.

"To Munga, of course. Ma will be shocked to see us arrive without notice. We must move quickly. Go pack your valuables, a few clothes for yourself and whatever else you think we might need for a reasonable length of time away."

He then wrote a short note to the Deputy Vice Chancellor, copying the Registrar, informing him that he was leaving the campus temporarily and asking him to act in his absence. He went out and handed the letters to the driver. "Give these to the Deputy VC and the Registrar", he told him. He went back in and began packing a small suitcase with some of his belongings. He waited a while for his wife to finish her packing. When she was ready, he put the cases into his private car and using one of the campus's perimeter roads and an obscure exit, drove out of the campus. He had lived through two other student disturbances since his appointment. This might be the final straw.

From his car's rearview mirror, he could see the road to the campus fading behind him, as he put an increasing distance between him and the university. It had been his home for four years.

Part 2
The Beginning

Chapter 6

Professor Malu Koney came to Manola, from North Western University in the United States, where he had been an African History professor, a position he was offered after serving a year at the university as a visiting Fulbright Professor. During the years he spent there, he earned a reputation for his oratory. His lectures were considered the most popular in his faculty. Apart from being one of the leading exponents of African history, he was an art lover and wrote extensively on African art forms and their relationship with indigenous African religions. The headhunt for a Vice Chancellor with outstanding academic credentials and a reputation for demanding high standards and discipline, ended with his appointment after six years of search.

He was born to Madika and Rose Koney. His parents relocated to Munga from Numbaya, a village in one of the country's provincial chiefdoms, soon after their first child Simfa was born. Madika had found it difficult to make a living working on his father's farm. So, when a baby arrived, he decided to leave the village and seek a better life for his new family. He convinced his wife that moving nearer to the city was the best option. He believed that the area held the greatest prospect for well-paid jobs. His sisters were already in the city, he told Rose. They would give them help when needed. When the couple arrived in Munga, Madika found work as a shop hand at a building material store. Rose stayed home to look after their young child.

As Madika gained the confidence of the shop owner, his earnings rose. Two other children were born. Ganeh, three years after Simfa, and, Malu, who came eight years after Ganeh, was an unexpected arrival. When Simfa was twelve, Rose's mother persuaded her to send Simfa for initiation into the local Dawa Womanhood society in Mumbaya, as was the family custom. Her father was opposed to this, but conceded for the sake of family harmony. As a young man, he too had been initiated into the male society at his home village and so were his two sisters, who were initiated into the womanhood society in their childhood. However, he felt that there were risks involved in the initiation rites, and so had not sent Malu and his elder brother Ganeh to be initiated as he was. He was living a different life, away from the old traditions of his hometown. In his new environment, he was determined to settle down with less imposition than there was back home. He had become an official of his church and served as an attendant at Sunday services. He was liked and respected by members.

It had always been Madika's goal to own a farm like his father had and work it more efficiently. As he earned more money he saved as much as he could, waiting for an opportunity to buy suitable farmland nearby. The opportunity came when Malu was two years old. Through friends he had made since settling in Munga, Madika heard of land and farm house for sale at Duru town, three kilometres from Munga. Madika seized the chance and bought the property. The sale was sanctioned by the headman who co-signed the receipt and transfer document. By then, Madika had worked in a local store for thirteen years. The store owner was sad to lose him. However, Madika had already set his mind on starting a business of his own and could not be persuaded to stay. Three months after the sale was finalized, and a year after negotiations started, he and Rose moved into the property with Ganeh, who was then 11 years old and Malu, who was 3. Their only daughter, Simfa had not returned from her stay with Rose's mother, so they were worried about her safety. They had heard nothing from Rose's mother since Simfa left for Mumbuya. There has been gossip around their neighbourhood, that something diabolical had happened but no one in the family could confirm or deny it. Rose had visited her mother twice, but could not find her or Simfa nor anyone willing to disclose their whereabouts. This had affected her relationship with Madika, but they had gone on holding on to their faith and believing that it was the will of God that they had lost their only daughter so mysteriously.

They farmed the land with a few hands, trying to make it the centre of their lives. Ganeh helped with house chores and during weekends and vacations did work on the farm under the supervision of the farmhands. When Malu was older, he took his turn on the farm, as his brother had done. For eight years, the family worked without interruption from anyone. Through their efforts and wise utilization of the land, they earned enough to look after their family comfortably. Malu entered Primary School at the age of four, just as Ganeh was about to take the Primary School Leaving Examination

(PSLE). The country was then experiencing political upheaval. Nationalist fervour was gathering momentum all over Africa. Some countries in the region had gained independence and others were moving towards that goal. In the case of his country, this had occurred five years earlier, in 1963. Many citizens had believed then that there would be greater opportunities for young people in a self-governing state than was available under colonial rule. There was high hope of prosperity, freedom, and justice for all. While the colonial government fomented ethnic divisions, and established artificial borders and land rights, a new self-governing state offered unity, peace, tolerance, and progress. The Koney's children and later generations stood to inherit a new country.

Ganeh did not like school and his parents could not get him to improve his attitude. When the results of the PSLE were announced, he scored too low a grade to get admission into any reputable secondary school. He refused to repeat the examination, or get a job, insisting that his father should endeavour to get him into secondary school, as other fathers were doing for their children who had the same grades. He began leaving home early and returning after dark. This went on for a few months. One day he did not come home. His parents put out notices at their church for information. They also reported their son's disappearance to the local police. All effort to find him failed. The disappearance caused more anger than shock to Madika. He always had concerns that their son would one day cause them unhappiness. It had a different effect on Rose. It distressed her. For years after the event, she kept pining for her son. She felt that it was her husband's often harsh treatment of the boy that had led him to abscond.

Malu became the only child in the house. On him, they laid their hope of reversing their seeming misfortunes. A painful period of soul-searching followed. Malu could feel the weight of sadness and dejection that hung around the house, but he treated it as a minor interruption in an otherwise stable environment. Unlike Ganeh, Malu was always on top of his class. He excelled in academic subjects as well as in sports. Slowly, the joy of receiving these impressive reports on Malu's performance at school, cooled Madika and Rose's anxiety over the fate of their family. Crying bitterly one evening, Rose fell at her husband's feet, denouncing those whom she felt certain had put a curse on their family. She believed that there was no other explanation for the loss that they have suffered.

A year on, the grief had eased. The buoyancy of the new business and the support from their church congregation, shut off the temptation for them to blame themselves and others for their situation. Malu was a gem. He was making them proud in a community that once had only pity for them. On the recommendation of the school's headmaster, Malu was made to take the PSLE a year early. He surprised even his teachers by scoring the second highest mark in the country. That automatically qualified him for admission to Clendon Boys High School, his first choice of secondary schools. When the results were announced at school, he ran home to inform his parents. They were out on the farm examining crops which were ready for harvesting. He dashed into the field of corn and found his parents weeding grass. Waving the sheet of paper bearing the school's notification of his results, he shouted, "Mama, Mama, I passed."

His mother rose from the heaps of red soil around her, singing with joy. She hugged him. "God is good, God is good!" she cried. She squeezed him so tightly, that he found it difficult to breathe. "Mama, I'm choking," he yelled. She put him down, still shouting praises to God. His father stood apart grinning with joy. Malu then ran to his father and hugged him too, saying gladly, "Papa, are you happy? I am happy. I can go to CBHS with the grades I scored. This is the school you want me to attend, not so Papa?"

"Yes, my boy, I am happy."

"Which of them is CBHS?" his mother asked.

"It is Clendon Boys' High School," he replied. "CBHS is the shortened form of the school's name.

"Mama, this is the school the pastor of our church went to," his father joined in.

"Is that so Papa? No wonder people from Bonoh town and others around here crowd into the church on Sundays to hear him preach. I was told that the greatest orators in the country had their schooling at CBHS. Anyway, I want to be a teacher." Who said?

"It is too early to decide. Many school children express interest at an early age in one profession and then switch to another as they grow up."

The excitement his parents felt was overwhelming. They abandoned their harvesting and went into the house to say a prayer with their son.

After prayers, they sat in the kitchen and watched Rose prepare their afternoon meal. They spoke about Malu's friends who had also passed the examination and wondered which secondary schools they would be attending. Malu told them about the school's plan to hold a farewell ceremony for the leavers and what each child should contribute.

"Why do we have to pay such money after we had paid those high school fees throughout your five years there?"

"Papa, that is how schools are these days. You must pay for every additional school function. "

"I am glad we have crossed this river," his father said. This is time to celebrate, not mourn over school charges.

A month later, a man from Clendon, who gave his name as Ayoma Donoteh, started visiting the farm. He accused the Koneys of illegally occupying it. Ayoma threatened to evict them from the land, if they refused to leave. Madika told the headman about these visits and the challenge to their ownership. The headman had assured them that there was nothing to worry about. He told Madika that he knew that the seller of the land, Jabe Kame, had lived on that land long before he was headman. even, since he was at school. "We know of no one from anywhere claiming the property since I became headman of this village," he told Madika. Madika's wife Rose, was also worried over these incidents and had told the wife of the farmer on the adjacent farm about their anxiety.

"Many people in the village know that Pa Jabe owned the land before he sold it to your husband," she said. "He and his son, who lived with him, had grown rice and pepper on part of the land. He had a small tin house on the land at that time and sold mostly palm wine, tapped from the palm trees on the land," she continued.

With these assurances, Madika and Rose ignored the threats from Ayoma, which were becoming embarrassing. On one occasion Ayoma arrived with a document signed by Jabe and his father, in which Jabe had agreed to carry out the duties of caretaker for the privilege of using part of the land to farm, until his father was ready to develop it. Apparently, when Ayoma's father died, Jabe illegally assumed ownership and sold it to the Koneys. Madika was furious and asked some of his farm hands to evict Ayoma forcibly for the property.

One day, Ayoma arrived at the farm with a surveyor and four burly neighbours in tow to confront Madika with further evidence of his ownership. He was ready for any violence that might erupt. He met Madika weeding his crops. He told him that he had no right to the land and that he should leave. He produced a copy of his title to the land from his briefcase and waved it in front of Madika's face. Madika was furious. While Madika and Ayoma were arguing over the document, Rose ran off into the town. When she saw the headman, she told him about the intruders on their farm. The headman asked several of his able supporters to accompany Rose to the farm and deal with the disturbance. They arrived at the entrance with cutlasses and sticks, shouting insults at the top of their voices, 'Where is the thief! *tifi tifi*' At the sight of the gang, Ayoma and his men found themselves outnumbered. He quickly put his document back in his briefcase and he and his men ran for their lives.

Two weeks later, a team of surveyors arrived with an official from the Ministry of Lands and a contingent of police officers. Madika and Rose were at their rice nursery with their workers, clearing weeds. The land's officer informed them, that his team was at the farm to conduct a survey. He said that it was part of an investigation of alleged dispossession of landed property by false means, brought to the attention of the ministry. Without waiting for a comment, he authorized the survey team to start work. Worried about the unexpected presence of officials on the farm, Rose hurried to the headman's office and asked him to come to the farm to resolve the problem.

When the headman arrived, the official told him that there had been a complaint from a man in Clendon, who said that the land which Rose and her husband were farming was his. He told him that the owner had been trying for a long time to get the unlawful occupiers to vacate the land. "I have here, Mr. Donoteh's deeds including the plan of the land registered at the ministry. He alleged that he owns this land and I am here to verify the boundary," the officer said. He emphasized that he and his men had the authority to act on the matter.

The headman put up a firm defence of the Koneys right to ownership of the land, though he knew full well he had been an accomplice to the illegal sale. "This is an unexpected violation of the rights of these hard-working people to peacefully farm on their land and enjoy the proceeds of their enterprise," he said with anger that convinced only the Koneys. He told the official that he felt insulted not to have been consulted before he approached Madika. "I am not here to deprive anyone of their livelihood. All I have been asked to do is to verify that the land, in area and location, as the one on the plan we have with us and registered at the ministry in the name of Ayoma Donoteh," the official said.

"We as headmen are also authorized to verify ownership and sanction sales in the villages, you know."

"That may be so, but ownership has to be confirmed by title deeds, which should include Ministry-certified land plans; otherwise rival claims could never be settled."

The Headman fought on. He shouted out, "Despite that, I can't stand idly by and see these good citizens deprived of their property so unfairly. Where was this intruder all these years, who now turns up as from the grave, to claim property in this village? We have never heard of any Donoteh family owning property here."

"That is not my concern. This matter seems to be in the hands of Mr Donoteh's lawyers and would eventually go to court, if there is no out-of-court settlement. There is a maxim you must remember for the future; 'buyer beware.' There is also the matter of threats of violence against an unarmed individual. No doubt, this will be handled as a separate litigation."

The matter went to court and the Koneys lost the case. On the charge of threatening violence, they were fined the equivalent of ten thousand dollars, in the local currency, which the Koneys could not afford to pay. Realising that they were victims of a fraud in which the headman had been involved, help and sympathy poured from friends and church members. Being one of the dedicated members of Munga Methodist Church in its glory days, the congregation rallied to help pay their fine and find them rented accommodation in Munga. Money was also raised to cover some of their post-eviction expenses. Though disheartened by their experiences they returned to working the parcel of land at the back of their rented house.

With conditions so dramatically changed for the Koneys, the possibility of Malu entering secondary school became uncertain. Sitting quietly on the back porch facing the house garden, Madika's thoughts strayed to events in his life that threatened to ruin his family. He wanted to cry, but forced back the tears, determined to fight through his difficulties. Malu and his mother walked up to him from the garden shed.

"Dad, you look a bit quiet today," he joked.

"I was only thinking about how we could find the money to get you into CBHS, with our present financial difficulties," his father said.

"Does that mean that I can't now go to secondary school?"

"I have been talking to our pastor about your future schooling and how he could help us. With the examination result you have, scoring the second highest grades in the country, I feel he will be more than pleased to help."

"Thank you, Papa. I am glad that I still have a chance to get into CBHS."

Madika stayed still for a while, as if unsure of what he had disclosed.

"God knows our case," he said. "He will make it happen. He has been our guide since we left our village to reside in this part of the country."

"Were there schools in your village in your time, Papa?"

"Sure, there were, but many families refused to send their children to them, because the only schools then established were by Christian missionaries and the lessons taught were in English. In those days, elders feared that the culture would be learnt with the language. That, they believed would bring in a different set of customs to their community. They had the same concerns too, when Islamic schools were introduced. Now we have three cultures, English, Arabic, and our African culture, co-existing in our community. A happy co-existence has been maintained for years now, but I fear the situation might change, if relationships turn sour in the future."

"That time will never come Papa. Our Civics teacher told us that all religions preach peace."

"That is my hope."

"Did your father send you to school?"

"Yes, my father sent me to the Sambu Clendon Church Primary School. He had joined the church when Christian missionaries established it in 1900. My two sisters and I went to that school, but they were sent to guardians in Clendon when the missionaries persuaded my father that they were too bright to have their education terminated at primary school."

"He must have been less worried than other families about his children being transformed into English children."

"Maybe that's so. But he took me out of school at the age of fourteen to work with him on his farm. The girls were luckier. Before he died, he saw them become teachers at one of the country's secondary schools."

"Your father must be pleased he sent them to school."

"Yes, but he still felt that the schools taught nothing about our history from early times; only other people's history."

Malu took the message seriously and wanted his father to know that he could improve the situation if he had the opportunity to do so. "Papa, when I finish CBHS, you can tell me everything you remember about our people and I will write them all down, so the family will have it saved for school children to read," he told his father.

"This will be better than telling these stories every time we have to pass them from one generation of traditional story tellers to the next. Often details of important events are lost in the process," his father replied.

Malu knew this already. His civics teacher had told his class once that some traditional story tellers make up parts of their stories to fit sections they had forgotten. In the end, different versions of the same incident are told by different story tellers in the same district.

51

"I want to be able to teach many things to school children. I will like that, Papa. If I am an orator too, that will help me teach more effectively."

Chapter 7

Malu's brother, Ganeh, left home at the age of thirteen After dropping out of school, he had found living at home intolerable. Since Madika could not send his eldest son to secondary school, he suggested that he find work as a shop assistant at one of the merchant stores on Market Street, as he had done. He explained to Ganeh, that he could work there until he was old enough to join the army, where there were opportunities for continuing his education. Ganeh told his father that he did not want to go into the army, but wanted instead to go on to secondary school and later become a mechanical engineer. His father told him that there was no money for that, but if he joined the army he could receive training towards that goal and earn money at the same time. His father could not stand his son's impertinence. He shouted him down. "Well, you better start believing that what you want cannot come from this house," he said. After a series of bitter exchanges between them, Madika told his son that if he had done better at school, he would have appealed to good neighbours to help pay for his secondary school education. "You believe that you can get what you want by doing nothing?" He asked pointedly. Ganeh was incensed. He told his friends later, that his dad's words hit him like poisoned darts, destroying the remaining cells of affection that he had carried. Ganeh felt that his father had condemned him in the most vicious way. His humiliation ignited a fury that forced a retort. "There are other ways of achieving my goal and I shall find one," he said and walked away.

Ganeh became disgruntled and refused to get a job, or work with his parents on the farm, while he looked for one. He took no interest in his parent's work. He hated the whole idea of farming, anyway. He thought that his father worked hard all the time, but still could not afford to give his family a decent life. He had long had disdain for the farm. When he was younger, his mother had encouraged him to work with her on the farm, during his spare time away from his books or on vacations, hoping that he would continue the business when they were too old to continue. Rather than joining his parents on the farm after finishing his homework, he preferred to be out with his friends, playing football in the street and chatting till late in the evening. He believed then, that the real money earners were footballers and champion cyclists.

Relations with his father gradually deteriorated, as Ganeh continued to distance himself from his parents. Problems with his father started when he was dropping behind in school. Madika had been firm in reprimanding his son. Ganeh had felt that his father was too hard on him, sometimes punishing him for what he thought were trivial things. He felt that his father did not love him. Rose tried to inspire confidence in her son, offering incentives for him to concentrate on his school work, instead of finding excuses for not getting decent grades. It made no difference to his performance. He loved football and that passion drove him to attend every club game played in the town.

During the month following the last bitter encounter with his father, Ganeh felt miserable and lonely. With no school to attend or serious job to pursue, he spent his day in the town's lorry park. He would leave home early in the morning before anyone was awake and return at night. He would make his way to the park humming his mother's favourite gospel tunes. There, he would help to unload trucks from the border towns, to earn some money. He was happy to have something to keep his mind away from his misery at home. He was not sitting and waiting for alms as his father would like to think. He was working with people from all walks of life, learning and taking chances. There were people involved in trade with neighbouring countries; transport operators and store owners. Those contacts he thought were all open to him now. One of those he met, was a man who owned a car repair shop at Kenge, some forty kilometres from Munga. Ganeh had helped him unload machinery and spare parts which the man had brought in for his business. The shop owner was impressed by the way Ganeh had taken care of his goods and put them together single-handed in one neat and secure pile.

Before he left the park, he gave Ganeh his address, and told him that if he ever had cause to visit Kenge in the future, he should call on him. "I will be too pleased to do that sir, particularly if you will offer me a job at your shop. I'd like to be a mechanical engineer," he had told him. The man had replied smiling. "You only need to get there, young boy," he said. This was too good too be true, he thought. His eyes glazed over at the opportunity.

Tensions at home continued. There was no easing of the strain, even with his long absences. Ganeh found the atmosphere unbearably thick with hurt. It was everywhere; hurt from dad, hurt from Mom, grimace from everyone who knew his parents. The house looked stranger than before the altercation with his dad. The cheery yellow paint on the sitting room wall seemed to have lost its brightness. The small room next to the kitchen, which was his bedroom, no longer looked welcoming. Every time he entered it, he sensed hostile feelings from everything in it?bed, windows, door, and the cupboard, high against the ceiling, where his Mum kept her clothes for special occasions. His bedroom furniture seemed to close in on him, making the room smaller than it was. He thought they wanted him gone. The master of the house was displeased with him, so he imagined perhaps, that they were complicit with him, teaching him a lesson for being stupid and unmannerly.

Unable to endure the tension in the house any longer, the young teenager decided to take up the the vehicle repair shop owner's offer. He packed what little he had and left early for Kenge. Ganeh's parents had become accustomed to his early disappearances from home and late return in the evenings, only to scrounge for food, and then disappear into his bedroom. He had been gone for five days when Rose went to get some goods she had stored in his room. She found Ganeh's bedclothes and some of his belongings missing. She knew then that she was about to experience another blight on her life.

Ganeh turned up at the Honda Car Repair shop, early the next morning. He had travelled on a bus from the lorry park and had arrived late in the evening. He spent the night in a guest house recommended by a passenger in the bus. The car repair shop owner was delighted to see Ganeh. He appointed him apprentice and handed him over to the head mechanic for guidance. He was found a room in the town, but soon moved out to stay with another apprentice, who had become his close friend and confidant in the shop.

After working for two years with few prospects of advancing in the trade, he and his friend began to look for other opportunities. They were earning too little to afford a decent living in a town that was growing fast. Its elegant residential area, the brightly lit shops filled with imported goods and the line of gem dealers' offices in the centre of town, showed off that wealth. One day, while he and his friend were at one of the Football Association's Inter-District elimination matches held in the town, they sat by a guy who had worked in the mines in Libesol. He told him how he had made large sums of money working as a mechanic in the gem mines. He said that there were companies looking for reliable mechanics to repair their bailing and electric generator machines. He said that he knew a friend who could put them in touch with one of these company bosses. They asked him to help them explore the chances of a meeting. He assured them that he would work on it.

Within three weeks Ganeh and his friend were fixing pumps and excavator engines in a mine far from home and country. The money was good and they kept most of it hidden in the shed they shared. Ganeh was happy that he had established himself. He had promised himself that he would make it in life and show his dad, that success can come from sources one never thought of before. "I have closed that man's chapter in my book," he told his friend. "Now, I have no father, no mother, no family. Just me, Ganeh Koney. He and his friend slowly found friends among other workers involved in the mining operations of the same company for which they worked. Some of them had been in the drilling and excavation end of the business for a long time. Others had been involved in processing the gems.

Relationships had strengthened between them, although many were from different countries and backgrounds. Soon Ganeh and his friend formed a small group of workers with like interests. They met during their regular week-end breaks, during which, they played card games and devised entertainment to relieve their boredom. On occasions, they travelled to the town centre to visit disco joints and clubs. On one of those visits, a guy in the group suggested that they resign from the company and form their own mining team. He told them that they had the collective experience to do it. "There is money in this business, I tell you. We all have so much to gain, if we proceed with the venture," he said. It was known that there were prospective mining plots available for rent by land owners. They normally received a share of the profit from the takings. He was willing to arrange this, he told them. They debated the proposal over many weeks when they were alone together in the mining camp. Eventually, they agreed to invest in the enterprise.

After the first unproductive season of mining, the group began to retrieve gems of minor value. Better luck followed and the business was as lucrative as they had predicted. With one mine exhausted they moved to another. Over time, new explorations became harder to find. Disappointment at the downturn hurt teamwork. Many of the partners lost most of their savings. Ganeh and his friend suspected that some cheating was going on, but could not prove it. Frustrated, they decided to form a new group. It took them a long time to get the new group up and operative. Ganeh was now well known in the business and was gaining respect from land owners and villages. Progress was good and as the years advanced, he and his friend set up home in the village and planned to live a settled life in the community that had welcomed them and given them the opportunity to prosper.

Chapter 8

As for Malu, he went to CBHS in 1960 with a scholarship from the Munga Methodist Church Trust. The trust was set up to educate bright children from poor homes in the town. Malu was always ahead of his class. At CBHS, he was so far ahead that he was promoted to a higher class after every mid-year examination, till he reached the highest class in the school. He took and passed the National Senior Schools' Examination at fifteen, gaining distinctions in all nine subjects. His performance won him a national scholarship to Clendon University, where he read History, Latin and Philosophy. In his final two years, he specialized in history. He graduated in 1974, with a Bachelor of Arts degree with first class honours. He stayed on at the university for another year to earn the Teacher Education diploma. After leaving Clendon, he applied for a teaching post at the Peninsula Secondary School. This he thought would keep him close to his parents.

He was appointed History teacher at the school in 1976. Two years later, he published his first book, entitled "Life and Times of the Galins." It was the history of one of the ethnic groups of the ancient West African Empire of Songhai. The book won him a Commonwealth Scholarship to pursue a PhD degree in History at the University of Durham and earned him royalty which he had paid into a savings account at the local bank, pledging never to touch it until he returned from his studies. When he came back home on completion of his studies, he was appointed history lecturer at the Kilinde Institute of Arts and Sciences (KAIS), in Marlon City, on the hills of Relfont. He paid regular visits to his mum and dad, who were so proud of him and looked forward to the news about campus life and his work at the Institute. Although his parents had lived fairly well from the vegetables they sold from their back garden, Malu felt compelled to improve their living circumstances. Withdrawing most of the money he saved up in the bank while he was away in Durham, he bought them a small house with a larger back garden. The family now had their own property. Over the following five weeks his parents worked hard to transform the house garden into a well-planned vegetable garden, with chicken pens and a tool shed. For the first time since they lost their property at Duru town, they felt happy and more relaxed.

Malu married Cecala Josola. The courtship lasted two and a half years, during which, he had to overcome his girlfriend's father's objection to their relationship because he favoured another suitor. His attraction to Cecala started at the Biennial Thanksgiving Service of the Clendon Boys High School. The School's Old Boys Association organized the service, although both present and past pupils attended. It was the tradition to invite representatives of the Old Girls Association of Clendon Girls High School, their female counterpart, to the service and to have one of the delegates read one of the lessons. At that service, it was Cecala who was asked to read the lesson, which was taken from the Old Testament scriptures. Her voice was clear and her diction impressive. Malu found not only her voice attractive, but everything about the reader. As they marched out of the church after the service, Malu kept looking back, searching for her, in the old girl's procession. He couldn't see her. A large number of old and present pupils marching behind him, blocked his view. When he was out of the church, he stood behind the church's grilled gate and waited for the old girls to troop out. Many of his old boy pals were beckoning to him to join them. He ignored their signs. "These chaps want you to indulge in empty talk to distract you from your own objectives," he thought. Patience rewarded him with her presence as she walked down the steps of the church. He waited until she was at the final landing before he moved from his watch post to meet her. He walked towards her and attempted to stop her with some flattering words. "That was an impressive reading from a formidable passage with all those jaw-breaking names," he said. She hesitated for a brief second and just brushed him aside to join her fellow delegates assembling at the footpath by the church's entrance.

The embarrassment showed in Malu's face as he retreated into the crowd of uniformed old boys gathering to start the traditional march from the church to the school's grounds. He vowed to continue his courting later, but then, he spotted a fellow female lecturer at Kilinde, Dr. Dametta Kailay. She was engaged in deep conversation with Cecala. He quickly excused himself from the crowd and walked over to the ladies.

"Dametta," he said to his colleague, "I didn't know that you were ex CGHS school girl."

"Many of you KAIS boys don't care much about us and still want to regard us as your school partners."

"That is not true. But I plead guilty. As you know, I have been away for some time and somehow lost touch with the tradition."

"Now you know the two groups of ex-pupils are expected to have each other's interests at heart, I hope I will have your support at the forthcoming Academic Board meeting when our department's proposal for a new course in Traditional Herbal Medicine is presented for approval."

"Surely you will have my support, but on condition that you introduce me to your friend here." He bowed towards Cecala, who was listening to the exchange between her friend and Malu. Dametta then turned to face Cecala.

"Cecala, this is Dr. Malu Koney." She then faced Malu saying, "Dr. Koney this is Miss Cecala Josola, my friend, and soul mate."

"It is my pleasure, Miss Josola," Koney said, offering his hand.

"Mine too, doctor," Cecala smiled as she replied. She took Malu's hand. They both pressed each other's hand lightly in a polite handshake.

"May I now be permitted to congratulate you on your word-perfect reading of the Old Testament passage at the service?"

"I am sorry I didn't stop to acknowledge your kind comments earlier. I didn't know you. Besides, I had been stopped so many times walking down the aisle, that I felt praising me for something I did often was unnecessary. You see, I teach at Sunday school every week and I am familiar with the Old Testament stories."

"My apology for being so abrupt. May I have the pleasure of making amends for my uncalled-for behaviour?"

"That will not be necessary. I accept your apology."

"Thank you, but I insist. Let me redeem the good name of my fellow old boys, by asking you to dinner tomorrow, or any other time convenient for you."

"Thank you, but give me time to think about it."

"Then I accept your judgement. Can I call you tomorrow just to talk? I assure you I will not be too much of a talkative."

"That's OK. My number is 030 536 723. I don't take calls during the morning hours, as those are the busiest times where I work."

"That's fine with me. I shall call you at six in the evening."

"Look here," Dametta said, interrupting the engaging conversation the two were having. She had stood by for a while as a harmless observer. "Malu! You are one daring man intruding into our space. In fact, your wings are not big enough to shelter this precious chick."

"How do you know that? Appearances are deceptive," he replied.

"OK, all I know is that you've derailed the happy train of conversation Cecala and I were having."

"My apology a second time," Malu said, "I must not cause any further offence. Till later, then." He left the ladies and walked back to join the men and boys already in position, to start the traditional march lead by the school's band. He found his position in the line of the decade of the sixties, feeling thrilled at having accomplished his mission. He marched joyfully, having only in his mind the prospect of talking to Cecala the following day.

Back at KAIS, Malu thought less of his promise to Dametta regarding support for her programme at the Academic Board, than for his promise to call Cecala on the phone. He called her telephone number several times over the following three weeks and took her out twice during that period. After their last date, he took her to dinner at the new Metropole Club on the Nesspa beach road. Since then, she had not answered his call. Malu felt that she was happy to be with him on that occasion. They even kissed as they parted at her doorstep. He thought that she was responsive to his suggestion to meet her again later that week. Concerned about the abrupt silence, Malu went to see Dametta at her office in the Department of Alternative Medicine. When he entered the office, he found her sitting behind a large desk. It was a large room. Two arm chairs faced each other in front of the desk. There was a book case to her right. Beyond the bookcase was an area set aside for important visitors. This was furnished with a two-seater settee and two lounge chairs. A coffee table stood conveniently in front of the settee. On the wall behind her, graduation photographs and certificates hung prominently, so that the first thing one saw on entering her room, was this array of testimonies to her earlier achievements.

"To what do I owe this honour, Malu?" Dametta said, rising from her seat to join him. They shook hands, then she kissed him on both cheeks. She offered Malu one of the seats in front of her desk. "Please sit," she said and took the seat in front of him. "You are welcome," she continued. He sat silently for a while taking in the room setting and deciding where to start. Then he said, "Is Cecala in town? She has not been answering my phone calls recently," Malu confided.

"That's strange because I spoke to her this morning. There was no indication that she had been away since we last met at the thanksgiving service."

"Would it be too much of an imposition if I asked you to find out why she has not been answering my calls?" Dametta looked down at her hands and up again. She looked at him. Her face carried the question before she said it.

"What on earth have I got to do with a relationship that is never going to get off the ground?"

"What do you mean?"

"Did Cecala not tell you she is already being asked for by a man named Abdu, from the Shefira family, who has majority interest in the Tonkolima mines? Her parents are keen on having their daughter married to him. She has been resisting this, but I fear she may have to capitulate if the pressure on her becomes too intense for her to ignore."

"So you are telling me to back off."

"Yes, if you are a wise man as you are made up to be."

"This Malu never puts his hand on the plough and turns back."

"This Kailay, can see further sitting down than any infatuated man standing up dreaming with his manhood sticking out of his pants."

"I beg your pardon."

"Excuse my frankness, but you might get hurt."

"Not if I can count on you to be on my side to fight this awful tradition of parents, having the exclusive right to decide to whom their children marry. It is like selling children in another form of slave trade. Forced marriages should be a thing of the past."

"It will be hard to stop, when it is taking place in the shadows, particularly in enlightened circles."

Malu rose from the chair as if to leave. He stood for a moment, looking as though he was going through some mental adjustment to the remarks he had just heard; then clasped his hands and sat down.

"Dametta," he said at last, "you have never heard of me fooling around with girls in or out of campus, like we hear of some of our colleagues. I am not one of those propelled to conquer everything that looks good in a skirt. Call it 'love at first sight' if you will, but I am in love with this girl. When we spoke on the phone, she was looking forward to our next meeting. I could sense in our conversation that she wanted to know me better. I want to give her that chance."

"I believe that there is a thing like 'love at first sight," she said. "I met my husband at university. The first time we met, it was I who fell in love with him. At that very moment I knew that this was the man I was going to marry."

"Lucky chap. I had no interest in developing filial attachments at university. You could say that I was one of those who felt that I had to stick to my books until the time was right for amoral distractions."

"Well, it paid off for you. You won all the academic accolades at every stage of your education, now you have to learn to win them out of university, searching for a partner."

"True and I will learn. This may be a fight that I cannot take on alone. Please join me."

"We already have an undertaking that you will fight my corner to get our department's proposal through the Academic Board. I can see myself joining with you in this fight too."

"Let's shake hands to seal this deal." He moved from his chair and took Dametta's hand, pumping it so hard, she had to shout, "That's enough, it hurts!"

"Sorry," he said. "It's the dreaming you mentioned earlier that has come upon me. Seriously, I am delighted that you are willing to help. That handshake for me confirms a lasting friendship, win or lose."

"Don't mention it."

"Come, let's sit over there in more comfortable seats, before I spell out the challenges we face." She pointed to the settee and armchairs behind her bookcase.

Dametta patted Malu's arm in a mark of encouragement to tackle whatever difficulties they might have to face.

"May I offer you a drink to cool your disappointment?"
"Water please."

She went into her office fridge and brought out a small bottle of Toots Spring Water for Malu and a regular bottle of Coca -Cola for herself. She placed two glasses on the coffee table and poured out the drinks. They sat together on the settee. No one spoke for a minute, then Dametta raised her glass. "Cheers," she said. They drank. She put her glass down, sighed loudly and began to speak. She told Malu about the situation in which Cecala was trapped. Her father was Works Manager at Dama Mines and had prospects of rising to a directorship of the board. Ten years ago, he was involved in an accident at the mines that left him badly injured. The Shefira family granted him early retirement with the best terms possible, in addition to full ride scholarships for his three children. All Gorbe and Shorbu Josola's children went to university and were in top jobs in government and industry. After graduation from university and further training in the School of Public Policy and Diplomacy, Cecala joined the Ministry of External Affairs as Assistant Secretary. Two months ago, her parents had called her into their bedroom after she returned from work and told that Mr. Kimara Shefira, his former boss, had visited them that morning. He had glowing words for her. He then told them that his son Abdu had been captivated by Cecala's beauty and poise for some time and it would please him greatly if they would consent to give their daughter's hand in marriage to him. "We shall be proud to have such a union between your family and ours," Kimara had said. Cecala's parents seemed to have been so enamoured by Kimara's request that they expressed gratitude for what he had done for their family. "Because of you our family is well respected in this society," they told him. They further made a promise to recommend the proposal to their daughter. Cecala heard them out and said. "Mum and Papa, we are no longer in a primitive age when daughters are sold to rich chiefs. I know how you feel about the Shefira and I am grateful for their timely support of our family, but Abdu is not my type. However, I will be foolish to cause friction between you and Mr. Shefira. Tell him that I need time to consider his proposal."

After telling all she knew, Dametta said, "Can you imagine how indebted the family must feel to the Shefira family for all that family had done for them? Now you have entered the scene, things get muddled further."
"A formidable situation for Cecala, I agree. Where do we start undermining this obstructive monument?"
"I think we have to plan this carefully. I'll work something out, trust me."
"That's great."
"I'll speak to Jezz about it and get something moving. Give me your contact number."
"067 354 009," Malu said.
"I'll be in touch." Dametta escorted him to the door.

Dametta informed her husband, Jezz, about her promise to Malu. Matchmaking was so far removed from her medical research skills, that she wondered how she allowed herself to get into it. But she was impressed by Malu's sincerity and felt compelled to make this match successful, regardless of the poor odds. She knew of many cases where parental insistence on choosing partners for their daughters have led to loveless marriages and their ensuing tragedies. She knew Cecala's situation well and how depressed she had been over the past two months opposing her parent's plan to get her engaged to Abdu Shefira. She had confided in Dametta that she had found Malu warm and engaging to be with. He had taken her out twice and she found being in his company relaxing. He had been a gentleman, not forcing himself on her. She wanted to go on seeing him, but feared her parents would disapprove of anything that might come out of their budding relationship, before the Abdu proposal was settled.

Dametta was true to her word. She got her husband's approval to host a dinner, as a pretext to bring Malu and Cecala together again. They agreed that they could do it in honour of Sima and Malitta Manleh, a couple who were married two weeks earlier. The bride's family and Dametta's parents were next door neighbours and they had been at the wedding; a subdued affair. When Dametta told Cecala that she was invited to the party, she was pleased to accept.

"I have met Malitta before. Both of us attend St. Charles at Relfont. I didn't hear of the wedding, but I am pleased for her. She is a very friendly lady," she said.

"You couldn't have heard. It was a quiet, low-key affair which took place at the Registrar's Office."

"No wonder. I notice that many couples are choosing the Registry these days; no doubt to avoid unwanted publicity."

"That's the way. I should tell you also that there would be another couple at the dinner, Jezz's mate at work and his wife. A friend of the newlyweds is also invited."

Malu received his invitation in a note which simply stated that Dametta and Jezz were hosting a dinner in honour of a newly wedded couple, and that they would be delighted if he would join them. He wrote back to accept, hoping that there would be an opportunity at the dinner to find out from Dametta how her intervention in the matter between himself and Cecala was progressing.

The dinner table was set for eight. The couple's six-year-old was already in bed when the guests arrived. Cecala was the first to arrive. Jezz ushered her into the sitting room and sat by her. Dametta heard her from the kitchen and rushed to welcome her. She gave her a handshake and a hug. Then dismissed herself. "Let me get on with my preparation in the kitchen, otherwise there will be no dinner," she said.

"Could I be of any help?" Cecala rose to follow her.

"No, darling. I have enough help back there. You stay here with Jezz to welcome the other guests."

It wasn't long after Dametta left for the kitchen, before the newlyweds arrived. They were followed by Jezz's workmate Albert and his wife, Adria. They had all been told 7.00pm was the time for dinner as. In Malu's invitation, Dametta had written 7.30pm. . Jezz led the new arrivals to the sitting room, introduced everyone and then served pre-dinner drinks. Soon after the arrivals, Dametta popped out of the kitchen and greeted the two couples. Jezz poured her a half-glass of ginger beer. She raised the glass. "Let's drink to the health and happiness of our newly married friend." They rose from their seats and drank the toast. She had a few words with the guests, then left for the kitchen, saying, "Dinner will be served in ten minutes. I hope you are all hungry."

The guests were called to the dinner table just after 7.25pm. "There is one more to come, but I think we can start," Dametta said. When Malu arrived, they had been served the first course. This was a bowl of fish balls set on a bed of fresh green salad.

"Come straight to the table, Dr. Malu. You are a bit late, but you will catch up on the service," Jezz said, although he knew that Dametta had planned it that way. Taken aback at the comment, he hesitated for a moment and then moved on. As he approached the table Jezz introduced him, "Hi friends, this is Malu Koney, a close family friend. Dametta pointed to the vacant seat on her left and opposite Cecala's. Malu greeted the other guests, then said to Cecala, "My God, what a surprise? How are you?" He offered his hand. She stretched hers and they shook hands." As they disengaged, he whispered in her ear, "Is this an apparition that I see before me?"

"Flesh and blood, I assure you," she whispered back.

At the other end of the table, everyone was in stitches, hit by the punch lines from Jezz's jokes. Dametta brought calm to the table by announcing that she was about to serve the main course. The used plates were passed down to her. She disappeared with them into the kitchen and returned with her house help to serve the second course. That was stewed lamb, fried rice and mixed vegetables. The final course of fresh fruit salad came after the married couple had asked for second helpings of the main course. Compliments were paid to Dametta for what the guests thought was a most delicious meal. Malu had avoided speaking to Cecala directly, since his first exchange with her. He rose and with all eyes on him, as he looked towards Dametta and said, "I like to start a round of toasts in appreciation of this great meal. "Ladies and Gentlemen, fill your glasses, and let's hear him," Dametta shouted across the table.

"To our fabulous hosts," he said.

Cecala toasted next. "To good friends and good company," she said, winking an eye at Malu, still in a standing position. Dametta took over from Cecala.

"I give this toast to all married couples," she said.

"Not fair," Jezz complained. Then he went on to say, "Here's to the blooming of relationship." Malu got up again. "That's abstract," he said. "Humanize it Jezz."

"*nosce te ipsum*; know thyself, if you understand me, that is."

The party erupted into laughter. That opened a flood of light jokes, which continued till the evening merged into the edge of midnight. It was the newlyweds who closed the party.

"May we be permitted to continue our honeymoon somewhere else?" Laughter erupted again. No one wanted to stay on after that appeal. Jezz and Dametta took leave of them on their doorstep, as they said their good byes. Before he left the table, Malu asked Cecala whether he could give her a ride home.

"Remember, this is an apparition. You may not be able to touch her," she said.

"I'll take my chances."

They drove off in his car with Cecala sitting on the front seat. Happy but confused, Malu didn't say a word to her for ten minutes. She pulled the reclining bar at the base of her seat and stretched back, her eyes closed, expecting, not expecting, to feel his hands touching her. "You've made an impression. She's been captivated." Those were the words of advice Dametta had given him as he left the party.

"Thanks." He nodded as if digesting her words.

Malu had thought of taking a scenic route to her house, but decided against it. When they were a short distance up the street from her house, he stopped the car and turned off the engine. "You are home," he said and kissed her cheek. She sat up, released the seat belt and to his surprise, turned around and kissed him on his lips, as lightly as the touch of a feather. Before she could withdraw, he held her firmly around her shoulders and kissed her again. It was different from the last. She moved closer, as he proceeded to explore the tender insides of her open mouth. At her suggestion, they moved to the back seat. He pressed the combination lock button and pulled down the rear windows three centimetres; no more. They squeezed into the narrow bench-like seat and lay side by side. Malu had his arms around her as Cecala nestled her head in the pit of his shoulder. He could hear her softly breathing; the breath of ease. "I love you Cecala, but you have been shutting me out."

"Not so. There's so much to tell, but can't just yet," she said. She blew out the words that Malu thought sent two different signals. One was that she had not shut him out. She was showing this by moving close to him till their bodies touched. The other was that she could not yet say that she loved him. But it showed, as she moved her hands over his delicate parts and kissed him in and on his lips with fiery intensity.

"I will wait," he said. "There will be no other than you for me." He could not see her eyes in the darkness of their makeshift love nest, but felt the wetness of her tears on his hairy chest. For him, she had spoken. He would have to wait until she chose to speak it aloud. At that moment under a moonlit night, it mattered not. They were together once again, alone and happy. They were pressed so tightly against the other, they could feel each other's hearts pounding against their chests. The night breeze drifted across the gaps in the back windows, cooling the heat generated by their bodies, as they sweat out their pleasure.

Chapter 9

Over the next month, Malu and Cecala met secretly. During that time, Cecala had visited her father's sister Mitu, and won her support in her fight against the Shefira proposal. Aunt Mitu told Cecala that it was ridiculous for her brother to have behaved in the manner he did, in an age of change. Cecala had spoken to her two elder brothers and discussed the Shefira proposal with them. They had supported her stand to reject it. She was now ready to confront her parents with her decision. One evening after work, she went into her parent's bedroom and told them that she had been seeing someone with whom she had fallen in love.

"I do not often disobey you, but I will not have Abdu as a husband." She said it calmly and added, "I will not change him for Abdu or anyone else."

"We will not accept any other man into the family. I am not going to be ungrateful to Kamira Shefira," her father said. He walked out of the room. When he left the room, Cecala said to her mother, "Mum, that attitude of Papa is the problem. I'd rather marry a man whom I know loves me, than one who would always feel that I was indebted to him. You must talk to Papa."

"Come here," she said to Cecala. Cecala moved over to sit by her mother on the bed. She put her hand on her daughter's shoulder and said "Your Aunty Mitu came to the house yesterday, to talk to your father and me, but your Papa was out at a church meeting. She promised to call again. Your father seems to have forgotten that his accident was caused by a faulty equipment which the mine owners failed to repair after mine inspectors had reported that it was dangerous to continue using it without repairs. We really don't owe him anything. However, your father sees it differently. He is a stubborn man; difficult to talk to."

Well, I have made up my mind. I am not marrying Abdu, nor any other Shefira." She shouted it so loud, that her father heard it and stormed back into the room. As he entered, Cecala walked past him into the sitting room.

Gorbe walked over to Cecala and stood in front of her. There was defiance written all over his face. He started with threats of violence against the man he thought was turning their daughter against them. Shorbu tried to calm him down. "Gorbe," she said calmly, "we have to treat this matter with a bit more compassion on all sides. I think we should care more for our daughter's happiness than for Mr. Shefira's. Cecala is no longer a child. She is an independent lady with independent means now. We cannot force her to think like us or do as we want. Times have changed. If you continue to pressure her to do your bidding, you will break the family. Her two brothers support her and so does Aunty Mitu. She was here yesterday and promises to be back. She and I spoke again this morning. She is annoyed with you. She thinks that you are gambling with your daughter's happiness."

"I don't understand all this fuss. In our tradition, girls or ladies, whatever their position, do not go out to find husbands on their own. Parents have that responsibility. That way the society keeps women protected from unscrupulous men." Shorbu pulled him to the edge of the bed and made him sit down. Once she saw that he was calmer, she said to him, "Gorbe, I think you should give yourself time to consider your position again. Keep an open mind for the time being and wait till we hear from Mitu."

Aunty Mitu visited the Josolas the following day. She was Gorbe's elder sister; an outspoken and fearless individual. She was tall and plump. Her solid figure told whoever intended to challenge her authority, that she was not one to be messed with. The visit went better than Cecala's mother had expected. Mitu informed Gorbe about the purpose of her visit. During their discussion, Mitu reminded Gorbe that she was the one who stood by him during the negotiations with Gorbe's employers; that she was the one who fought for him to get the favourable early retirement terms from Shefira Mines Corporation, which he now enjoyed.

"It was not a simple matter to get the company to agree to the terms we got for you. Don't you remember that we had to threaten the company with court action before a deal was finally struck?" Mitu told Gorbe. "Now," she continued. "I want to hear nothing more about a Shefira wedding. You must let Mr Shefira know that you have consulted your family, and that they have taken the decision not to accept his son as a suitor for your daughter."

"I cannot face him with such a rebuff," Gorbe said, remembering that he had given his former boss the impression that he was in favour of such a union.

"If you cannot, I will," his sister said.

"Mitu, this matter is my affair, so you must stop meddling."

"It is our family's affair also. Cecala is my goddaughter, remember? It is also my responsibility too, to see her happy in marriage. You and Shorbu should quickly let Shefira know by which ever means you choose, that the family has other plans for Cecala."

Feeling defeated, Gorbe left his seat and moved over to sit by his sister.
"Sister Mitu, it will be difficult," he said. "But everyone in the family seems opposed to the match, so I have to fall in. Will you join Shorbu and me to pass on this decision?"
"That sounds like a sensible man speaking. I will be delighted to. Just let me know when you want me."
"I will invite him here and make sure I give you plenty of notice for the encounter."
"I don't need a long notice. I'll come even at an hour's notice."

A day after Aunty Mitu's visit to the Josolas, Cecala paid her aunt a visit. She told her aunt that she would like to introduce Malu to the family, if she could soften her parents to the idea. It took Aunty Mitu two weeks to arrange the family gathering, which took place in a spirited atmosphere. Aunty Mitu was the grand conductor of affairs. The expected guest arrived when the immediate family were all assembled. Cecala spoke quietly. "This is Dr. Malu Koney," Aunt Mitu said, as Malu walked in. She continued more loudly now. "I would like you to accept him as my special friend and one that I have developed a deep liking for." She told them about Malu's humble background and his achievements. Her father remained quiet most of the time, taking in whatever he could read from this stranger's face and manner. In the end, he said, "You seem a serious fellow, son. However, I need to let you know that Cecala has been a good child to us. We love her. She has been the one living with us now and looking after us. I expect you to be proper in your dealings with her."

Malu was in no doubt what proper meant to a man steeped in the traditions of his ancestors. He remembered his humble background and how that made him vulnerable to accusations of being a social climber. He stood up to reply. He wanted to be angry at the condescending tone of his remarks and wanted to defend his integrity, but knew that anger was no option at that moment. This man was going to be his father-in-law, whether he liked it or not. He had to swallow his pride. . Cecala sensed the pressure of the conflicting thoughts weighing on his mind. She left her seat and stood by him. She put her arm round his and squeezed it mildly. She could feel the tension in his body slowly easing. It was like giving him a tranquilizer shot. It steadied him. Looking directly at his father-in-law seated in the middle of a row of family members, he began to speak. He spoke aloud with all the eloquence he could muster. "She means so much to me, Sir," he said calmly. "I am just starting out on a career at the Kilinde Institute of Arts and Sciences, so, I have no claims to riches, but be assured Sir, that Cecala will be in safe hands. I will love her to the end of my own life."

His mesmerizing words gripped his audience's attention like the force from a conjurer. He had proved himself to the family and they showed it with smiles and hugs. It took another two weeks before the Josolas could call the Shefiras to receive the family's verdict on their proposal. It was a stormy meeting, but Aunty Mitu delicately steered the gathering to a safe landing. She convinced Kamira Shefira, that she and her brother's wife had done all they could to persuade Cecala to accept his proposal, but found it impossible to overturn the relationship she had formed with another man before his intention was known. Cecala and Malu received the news of the rejection with elation. They no longer had to deal with the threat to their relationship, from a man whom Cecala had met only once at a company fair when she was ten years old. They wasted little time, but planned visits to friends and family. When they visited Malu's parents, they were pleased that their son had at last found someone with whom he could settle down.

Two weeks later, Malu's parents paid a visit to Cecala's home. The visit was arranged by Cecala. That was a successful visit. The Josolas welcomed them warmly. Cecala's mother had prepared a light meal for the guests. Cecala's brothers were invited to meet their prospective in-laws. They brought some light-heartedness to what would have been a dull occasion. Throughout the visit the brothers kept teasing their father about losing the jewel in his crown. Malu was more relaxed than at his first meeting with Cecala's family. During the visit, both families agreed all arrangements for the engagement rites and the wedding ceremony. The wedding took place on

April 20th 1978 at the Munga Clendon Church. The couple settled down to a new life at Horton. Malu was no longer a bachelor. Invitations to functions they hosted on campus would carry the titles 'Dr. & Mrs.' Dametta and Jezz became their most trusted friends.

Malu's years at the institute were marked by outstanding academic achievements. He rose to the position of Professor at age thirty, served several terms as Dean of the faculty of Arts and two terms as Vice President in charge of student discipline, college maintenance and environmental matters. He was known for his great oratory. Students admired him and his peers respected him. He was university orator for five years. During those years, he would invite his parents to every graduation ceremony when he was to present candidates for the award of honorary degrees. His father would glow with pride as his son spoke. From time to time he would lean over and touch his wife. "That's my boy, a true High School boy." He would then turn to look at the rows of guests behind him as they erupted with applause.

Because of his outstanding academic and administrative record at the institute, he was considered one of the likely academics to succeed the president, when he retired from office. By the time the president was due to retire, Malu was still young for the post, considering the average age of those who had held the post in recent years. So, when six months before the president was to retire, the institute's governing council appointed a search committee to prepare a short list of candidates for the post, some of the older academics were surprised that he was on the shortlist. There were two other names on this list. The interviews were conducted over a three-month period. At his interview, Malu thought that he had performed impressively. He believed that he had put enough of his charm into the discussion with the panellists, to sway them to his side. At 41, he would be the youngest President since the appointment of the first African to the post sixty years earlier. That was not a consideration for him. He believed he had the dynamism and intellect to maintain or even excel the achievements of past presidents.

There would be weeks before the committee could make a recommendation to the governing council. At the latest, an announcement was expected a month before the present president's contract ended. As the interview process went on, rumours spread like wild fire on campus, giving details of the committee's proceedings. It was revealed that during the first round of interviews, the shortlist was narrowed to two; Malu Koney and Salac Fanda. Fanda was a renowned scientist, who had been at Kilinde for over twenty years and known for his disdain of young lecturers who advocated for changes in the administration of academic departments and in regulations which hindered innovation in many spheres of KIAS's academic life. Unlike Fanda, Koney was the idol of the young lecturers. He supported their ideas and defended their course in Senate and Council. After several more sittings, the committee was unable to agree on a candidate to present to the governing council, as they found both candidates equally qualified and competent to succeed the retiring president. Curiously, they took the decision to submit to council the two candidates left on the shortlist, asking that body to make the choice between them. When the committee's report was ready, the governing council held an emergency session a day after the report was received, to limit leaks of its contents. Being a candidate in contention, Malu and Fanda were not permitted to attend. However, some of Malu's supporters attended, as Fanda's did. At that meeting, members also failed to reach a consensus and had to resort to a vote.

Immediately following the meeting, Malu's supporters drove to his residence, to report the outcome of the meeting. They were loyal friends; all senior academics. For as far back as he could remember, they had always sought each other's interests. They knocked on the door and waited. Malu opened it and ushered them into his sitting room. He was alone in the house. His wife, who was pregnant with their third child, was away in Clendon seeing her doctor. "Mal," they said, as they walked into his sitting room and sat on chairs around the room. Mal is the way his close fiends fondly referred to him. "The news is not good," they said. "Salac Fanda got it by a simple majority vote," one of them said. For over a week prior to the council meeting, there had been rumours s about clashes between members of the search committee and the chairman, who was said to be biased in favour of Funda, but that most members favoured Malu.

It was shocking news for Malu. . His friends looked at each other and waited. He did not respond. After a brief silence, one of them spoke. "I am not surprised," he said. "Council preferred to appoint someone it could manipulate, not one that would stand up for principles and refuse to violate codes of academic practice which keep institutions in the highest academic leagues in the world." He moved over to sit by Malu. Crossing his arms, he explained how the voting went. "Many of the representatives of the Academic Board in council were outvoted, their votes swamped by appointed members," he said. Malu looked dazed, as words of consolation were offered to him. It took some time before he was back to some consciousness. Then he said quietly, "Thank you chaps for bringing me the news. The contest is over, I lost. I think I am strong enough to weather it. I shall have to tell Cecala; it was not what was expected."

His wife had been receiving visits from many friends who had encouraged her to believe that her husband would be appointed the next president. Malu knew that the news would devastate his wife. His friends stood up. No one wanted to speak. They knew that it would be counterproductive to continue to console him. To their surprise, Malu rose to join them. "Thank you again," he said. "No thanks," one of them said. "This is only a minor setback. In 10 years, Salac would be gone," he told him. They all knew that the institute's conditions of service limited presidents to two terms, each of five years' duration. "You are only 41," he said. "You will still be eligible for appointment at 51. That has been the ages of most of the former presidents on their first appointment. Salac is 53." They joined hands together, in a spirit of brotherliness, sharing his disappointment. As they dropped their grip, he said to them, "I shall have to consider my options later. Now let me lick my wounds. Besides, I have a christening to attend in Munga tomorrow."

His friends left, feeling a strange tenseness that would define a new relationship between him and them.

Part 3
The Fallout

Chapter 10

Malu woke up tired the next morning. He couldn't sleep well all night, thinking about his future. Yet, he had an engagement to keep; the christening of Dr. Radel Lamara's daughter at 10.30 am that morning in Munga. He was one of the godfathers to the child. Malu and Radel had been childhood friends. They had attended the same Primary and Secondary schools together and had maintained their friendship throughout their professional journeys. He had promised Radel he would attend. Furthermore, he wanted to tell his parents that things had not gone well for him at the emergency meeting of the institute's board of governors the day before. He showered quickly, put on appropriate attire for the occasion and dashed to the dining room to have a snappy breakfast. Cecala had woken up early to prepare breakfast and was bringing it to the dining table, when Malu came out from their bedroom, heading for the table. She placed on the dining table, a bowl of corn meal and generous slices of roast plantains.

"I will not be going with you to the christening as I had planned," she said, bowing her head, to avoid eye contact with her husband.

"Why darling, we don't have to be there all day," he said, forcing down a spoonful of the meal. "We only need to show our faces and then disappear," he continued.

"Not when you meet your friends and start talking, especially those you have not seen for a while."

"Not this time. I am too emotionally drained today to indulge in reminiscences."

"You say that here. I know Alinse will be there. He is full of yarns. He never allows anyone to leave his company when he is in his element. Apart from that, I'd like to give ourselves space to reflect on our disappointment."

"Don't worry about me. For goodness sake Cecala, you need to get it off your mind and concentrate on keeping healthy for the sake of the child you are carrying. I lost the job. It is finished." He knew that he was shielding the truth. He too was heart-broken.

Since Malu had shared the news with his wife , she had found it difficult to sit with him or talk about it. That was the way she had decided to deal with the disappointment.

She moved away from the table and disappeared into their bedroom.

Left alone, her husband sat quietly for a while and then rose from the table, leaving most of the food untouched. He walked to their bedroom and knocked on the door. "I am leaving now," he shouted. "Have a safe trip," she replied.

It was a voice that had sadness all over it. She had been crying. The disappointment had hit her like an arrow, piercing her pride and killing her hope of becoming first lady of the campus. He knew that she was distraught. Suppressing his own feelings, he turned the door knob and entered the room with a phoney smile to break the ice . She had their youngest child, Abi, lying on her right side; her hands around her mother's neck, her cheek pressed against hers as if sharing her mother's grief. He moved to the other side of the bed, touched her cheek lovingly, and then kissed her and his daughter. "I will be back as soon as I can," he said, shutting the door.

He drove out of the campus at 8.00 am, allowing time for delays on the road. He took the road into the city. Fifteen minutes later he was driving eastwards out of the city through Netway Road. He joined the main highway , avoiding the mountain road, which was a shorter route to Munga, but it had dangerous hair-pin bends and steep gradients. Besides this, its surface had been in a bad condition since the last rains, which washed out some embankments and reduced the road in some sections to a single lane. Malu decided that it was safer to use the main highway, which linked the capital city to the rest of the country. It was reconstructed, fifteen years ago, to provide a high quality all weather road to withstand the heavy traffic using the route. On a quiet day without traffic, it would take only an hour to travel from his home to Munga. Malu was hopeful that it would be one of those quiet days.

The highway is a four-lane dual carriageway for part of its length. On reaching the outskirts of the city, the carriageway narrows to a two-lane road. The congestion caused by this sudden reduction in traffic often caused chaos that the traffic police had never been able to control. This part of the city has its own unique character. Shops of all kinds line both sides of this cramped road. They compete with maintenance garages and traders, who erect stalls in front of their entrances, sometimes extending them to the edge of the narrow footpaths. Across these narrow kerbs, petty traders spread out their wares in defiance of the police. Goods of every description; pots, pans, cutlery, crockery, electrical goods, patent medicines and medicinal herbs, sit dangerously in spaces car mechanics have left unoccupied. In spaces, they have captured for their vehicle repairs, massive pollution had occurred. Discarded engine oil from repaired vehicles flood the pedestrian passageway. Dumped on sections of this black menace, were mounds of decomposed food scraps and other household rubbish, cleared from adjacent roadside drains and deposited on the degraded walkway, accentuating the filth of these areas. The unsightly spectacle had marred the otherwise impressive view of the line of new buildings erected in this eastern fringe of the city. The stench from these heaps filled the air, making breathing of its noxious ingredient a health risk to be avoided. So, wise passersby pinch their noses to restrict breathing while they sped past these dangerous obstacles. Not one of the polluters is ever called to account for damaging the environment. So, they leave the ground around them, transformed into mounds and craters of filth. It was clear that the continued use of the nation's sidewalks for the repairs of motor vehicle, would cause irretrievable harm to the nation's health and infrastructure objectives.

Although it was a Sunday, the area was bustling with activity. Large groups of people had assembled on both sides of this cramped road and in front of shop doors. Excitement glowed on their faces. There was an expectation in the air. Standing in the crowd in front of Sita's Hair Salon, a young man moved forward at the sound of a hunting horn. There were three short blasts, a signal he alone understood. He moved nearer to three other men in the crowd. They were dressed in the same red and white outfit that he was wearing. They carried red flags. Whistles hung conspicuously around their necks. The young man had noticed something the others had not seen. "They are coming," he said, spinning around, and looking to his left. There was a man in the same outfit as his and his friends', signaling to him from the front of a palm tree at the junction of the main road and the dirt track leading to Oyster Wharf. "Let's get ready," he shouted to his mates and together they pushed through the crowd and entered the roadway, blowing their whistles, and waving their flags. The outbound traffic from Clendon came to a halt. The men took various positions on the road to halt the traffic until they had created a large area empty of vehicles. Their mission accomplished, they blew their whistles again and out of the dirt road, a procession of dancers led by a masked '*Ebon devil*' emerged. They swayed to music from drums and flutes as they moved into the makeshift arena. The dancers filled the space and within a few minutes of display were rewarded with thunderous applause from the crowd. The ecstatic crowd burst into the arena and joined in the dancing. In the middle of the crowd, the masked devil somersaulted and displayed other acrobatics, which pushed other dancers and spectators into a ring around them. Angry drivers sounded their horns in protest, but no one absorbed in the exotic performance on the highway cared. The dancers held up the traffic for nearly half-an-hour before the police was called to clear the road. Reluctantly, the show left the highway and moved into a clearing on the opposite side of the road.

Malu joined the long traffic queue at a point, a hundred metres from the entrance to the former Nabom factory estate. It had been closed for nearly 5 years, but the estate remained an imposing landmark. He looked at his watch. It was 8.40 a.m. The christening was to start at 10.00am. "Hope I can make it on time," he thought. He had expected to arrive in Munga in time for the christening service. He had left home early enough to make it , but the journey was taking longer than planned. He assessed his chances of reaching the church on time. "If I can get out of this traffic jam before nine o'clock, I might just make it," he thought. Still unruffled, he leaned back on his seat. The traffic ahead of him was not moving, even a metre since he joined the queue. In the cramped roadway, ordinary pedestrians and hawkers skilfully navigated gaps between cars. Through these tiny spaces, hawkers wriggled to offer frustrated drivers and passengers comfort. "Cold drinks to cool you? Biscuits?" a young hawker shouted. He was ahead of a line of sellers displaying their goods and struggling to make sales against stiff competition. In the distance, the sounds of other hopefuls in the trade, advertised their wares, all unrecognizable in their fast recital of their trade chants. He could make out one round of chants "Fancy towels for your beautiful home! Table mats and napkins! *Gara* and Raffia types! Try Tiger Bone pain killer; Mobile phone chargers! Top up! Top up! Top up for your mobile phones!" More shouts, less distinct, came through from other sellers, "Magic Mosquito

Coils! Masquita spray! kills masquita dead fast. Bitter Cola! It makes men true men! (no doubt an *aphrodisiac*). Pop Out, best rat poison! Tapalapa bread to keep hunger away *tay go!*" The chants rose to a crescendo as the sellers moved closer to Malu's car. It drowned the idle beat of engines in cars with air conditioners. Many of those within them had shot out the heat and sellers' sounds, and were lounging undisturbed in the cool air of their temporary jails.

The traffic jam now stretched for two kilometres behind his car. Ahead of him, the queue extended 500metres to where the highway narrows. His car was on the outer lane of the dual carriageway section, in an area of the road where many side roads meet the outbound carriageway. Feeling frustrated in his marooned car, he chanced a look in his car's rear view mirror. There, 400 metres behind him, was a bridal car with a wedding entourage of six vehicles stuck in the traffic. To his amazement, everyone in the cars in the entourage, were out trooping up and down the queue pleading and cajoling drivers to make a passage for their vehicles. Eventually, they were able to open a narrow channel for the bridal fleet to pass through. It took nearly forty minutes for the gaily decorated cars to leave the highway, taking the nearest exit. That effort might have ensured that a wedding event took place, but surely not on time.

Malu knew he had no chance of receiving such favours, as did the weeping bride at risk of failing to turn up at the event of her life. The courtesy shown to the wedding party was not shown to vehicles from the side roads either. They had been stuck at every junction, trying to enter the outer lane of traffic. Drivers on the highway were unwilling to give way at these junctions, for fear of losing their positions in the queue. At every one of these junctions, scuffles were breaking out. Drivers were jumping out of their marooned cars and confronting those blocking their entry into the traffic stream. Viewing this disorderly scene and the further delays it might cost him, he began to regret the decision he made to take the urban route instead of the mountain road. "I could have avoided this mess and taken the mountain road. That would have taken me to Munga by now," he thought. Stressful situations trigger awkward thoughts, some unhelpful. He now saw the use of the mountain road as a preferred option. Its danger had become less of a concern to him.

By the time he reached the junction, where the mountain road joins the main road, it was already 10.00 am. He knew that the service had started. He would be late. Despite all the risk he took, exceeding the speed limit to overtake vehicles on the road, it took him another thirty minutes to arrive at the church. He walked into the porch way but hesitated to enter. The church was crowded. Every seat seemed to have been taken. The town had come out in support of their doctor. Invited or not, many residents felt they had to be there. Radel Lamara was popular in the town. He had been a consultant physician at the Clendon Hospital for nine years, before resigning to set up the Lamara Clinic at Manda Street. He had developed it as a private health facility, providing badly needed health care for citizens living in the area. Before the facility was established, town folks were given the privilege of receiving treatment at the military hospital at the Munga Barracks. However, treatment of non-military personnel was limited to Mondays, Wednesdays and Fridays, between 8.30 am and 3.00pm. Outside those times, the sick sought treatment from pharmacists in drug stores on the main road, or from traditional healers in near-by villages. The incidence of avoidable deaths was high before Dr. Lamara established his clinic in the town. There was now a significant drop in those numbers. His presence had made a difference to the ad-hoc health situation in the area.

"Come with me, Sir," a church attendant said politely as he approached him from the inner hall way. He directed Malu past fully occupied pews and raised eyebrows, to the two front pews which had been reserved for sponsors, close family members and friends. Aunty Macile and Aunty Banie his father's sisters were invited to the christening and were seated on the second row behind the Lamaras and their immediate family. His aunts made space for him between them. The wings of their exotic head dresses framed his chubby round face and made him look like an intruder, peeping through a parted screen. He found it difficult to concentrate on the service. His mind drifted out, then in, then out of the church again. It took him to his father, whom he must see and let him know his plight and then to his wife, about whom he worried. He was concerned about the condition in which he had left her. She did not want to be at the christening, which they had planned to attend together. It was clear to him that she had no intention of attending any function, where she would have to face people who knew that he had failed to get the President's post and would want to offer commiseration. She wanted no one's pity. A nudge from Aunty Banie brought him back to a presence in the house of God, but he was seeing nothing but blankness. He drifted away again. He imagined entering a new life; one of uncertainty. "What was his life going to be like from that point on?" He was framing questions, hard questions for which there were no ready answers. Failure for him was as bad as not being shortlisted. He knew what the panel was looking for, and he gave it to them with his trade-mark fluency. Was that the end of the road for his career?" Many more questions crowded his mind, making little sense in the senselessness of the battle he was fighting within himself.

Though Radel was baptized a Methodist, the baptism of his child took place at St. Mark's Anglican Church, almost opposite Munga Methodist Church, where Malu and Radel were christened. They had attended service there with their families for years until they finished secondary school. Malu and Cecala were married there. The church was now a relic of its former grandeur. Only two external walls of red laterite stone remained. Their tall and imposing form, dominated the deserted plot where debris of every kind lay hidden in thick *lalan* grass. Some of the congregation of the church had long since found permanent spiritual shelter at St. Marks. The others had been attracted to the variety of evangelical churches that had sprung into life since the demise of Methodism in the town. Malu's parents now worshiped at Okeju Evangelical Church. Town folks were amazed that the Methodist Church could allow this dilapidation to take on such a regretful permanence. In most of the districts around Munga, Methodist Churches had suffered similar fates, succumbing to neglect. The Anglican Church had done much better in maintaining their churches in these areas. As far as worship centres were concerned, Munga had too many for such a small town. But as the situation was, the fate of the Methodist Church in the town was sealed. It might be difficult to bring back lost members or attract worshippers from among the young generation of Christians, even if the old church was rebuilt. Young people had relished the fervour and exhibitionism in evangelical church services so much, that once hooked, they stayed. None had ever considered leaving to go back to the old established churches of their ancestors.

"Will the parents and sponsors please come forward with the child to be baptized?" The officiating minister announced with arms stretched out ready to receive baby Minke. The parents and sponsors moved from the pews and walked gingerly to the altar. Malu walked behind one of the godmothers. Her trim figure clamped in a tight floral dress, emphasized the swings of her rounded hips. She was tall, her jet black hair tied in loose plats fell lazily behind her neck. There was something in front of him that woke him from his dreamy state. His eyes followed the sensual movement. This was a body he would love to explore, if given a chance. He wanted to see her face and read her emotions. Lust had replaced disappointment. They reached the altar and she walked on to stand by the child's mother and other female sponsors. He wanted to go on and stand next to her, but saw that the other godfathers were standing next to the child's father. Unsure of what the protocol was for such occasions, he joined the line on the father's side. The formalities at the altar were brief. Nearing the end, the sponsors were asked to repeat after the minister, their pledge to bring up the child in accordance with Christian principles. His mind had drifted again. No one noticed that his lips were closed while the others spoke. He had promised nothing. As they moved back to their seats, the baby's mother leading, Malu tried to catch the eye of the girl whose rear had excited his manhood, but it was she who turned around and fixed her gaze on him for a brief second. Then she walked quickly on.

Malu took in a snap view of her. His eyes registered a face that complemented the form of what seemed to him a beautiful body. Against the stretched fabric of her stunning dress, her upper frame bulged slightly outwards in contained elegance, making her side view more titillating than the rear. It was her eyes that had the alluring glint, but Malu did not have the roaming streak. Philandering was out of his character. His life was dull and regulated, given mostly to academic research. What little time he had to spare, he devoted entirely to his family and to the occasional squash game with his friends. He looked away from the charmed eyes that mesmerized him and drawing him to attempt the climb up the tricky slopes of infidelity. For a moment, he stood still as blankness replaced the enticing image. He allowed the other men to go ahead of him. They did not see his lips move. This time he was silently talking to God.

"O Lord," he said, "save me from myself. The arrows of temptation are directed towards me. Let me not fall a victim to them and compound the shame I now face."

He began to move forward slowly. He did not know how he reached his seat beside his aunts. He bowed his head on the back of the seat before him. In silence, he prayed again. When he sat up, a feeling of unusual calm eclipsed him. He thought that in a way, he had been redeemed from his guilt.

Chapter 11

After the christening service at St. Mark's, guests of the Lamara family accompanied them to their home for refreshments. The family had made sure that there would be more than enough food and drinks for their guests. The dining and living room area had been combined to form a large hall, which was decorated tastefully. Tables with matching chairs were arranged in rows as in a restaurant. There was a setting of tables and chairs in the back garden to accommodate the spill over of guests from the house. The room was packed full of guests. The atmosphere was cheerful. Many of the guests had been seated when Malu arrived. He found a seat at a table with four old friends. Their table was near the entrance to the back garden, from where they could see the colourful garden decor and the spread of guests under bright yellow canopies. At the table, nearest to theirs, were some young men talking so loudly and almost at the same time, that they were becoming an annoyance to guests sitting at tables close to them. Everyone on Malu's table could hear the rambling going on next to them. For his part, Malu felt uneasy seated so close to this boisterousness around him. He made several attempts to leave; each time, his friends successfully found ways to stop him leaving.

"The noise is part of the fun," one of them said.

"I agree," Alinse added. "Mal, you can't go, we've not been together like this for years. We need to catch up on our past." He spoke for others on the table, using the nostalgic line.

"I have little to tell." Malu said. "Same old job, teaching the next generation of leaders," he volunteered to speak first.

"We know about your achievements Mal. We are proud of you," Alinse commented, while Malu looked pensive. He worried that he might be asked about happenings at Kilinde. It did not happen. The rest of them gave their stories.

Alinse Brosna, was a senior lecturer at Bundama Teachers' College. He spoke of incidents at the Clendon University when he and Malu were students there. They shared a room at Mansa Hall in their first year. He had studied Philosophy and Modern Languages. After leaving college, he spent three years as a teacher at the Prospect Secondary School in Clendon before his appointment as Lecturer in French at Bundama. The youngest in the group, Manga Bikolo stayed in Munga after finishing primary school. He went on to secondary school there. On leaving school, he joined his father's construction business in the town. He had been running it successfully for the last five years, since his father died in a road accident.

At the end of the round of briefings, all drank a toast to their past and future successes. Malu drank the toast with a half glass of Coca Cola, then breathed a quiet sigh of relief. No one in the table knew about his university problems. "It was time to leave," he thought. "Chaps, I must go now, I've got to see my Pa," he mustered the courage to say it. The men were having fun, drinking and laughing. It seemed strange to them that he would want to leave such a happy reunion.

"Not now Mal. The food service is nearing our table. Why don't you wait till we've eaten?"

"I don't really feel hungry, Mal said. "I was up too early this morning. My system is not yet functioning properly." He could not tell them the real reason for his system not functioning properly.

"It is just after noon. You should have gotten over it by now," Alise teased.

"A shot of brandy will clear that." Alinse reached for the bottle of Courvoisier among the collection of drinks laid on their table and opened it. He took the glass in front of Malu and held it, ready to pour some out into the glass.

"No! You don't! I don't drink," Malu said, reaching over to stop him. He was too late. Alinse had a good 50 ml of the tawny liquid poured already into the glass before he could snatch the bottle from him.

"Sorry Mal," Alinse said. "I didn't know you don't indulge. They say a drop of alcohol from time to time is good for the system."

"Not mine old chap. In any case, no one with an ounce of medical knowledge, has a good word for that tongue-scorching, addiction-forming drug."

"I understand that it is a medical fact that alcohol opens the arteries and increases the blood flow through the body." Alinse was eager to justify the disappearance of the contents of so many cans of Carlsberg beer lying empty on the table.

The conversation was drawing Malu into an area he felt strongly about. He felt obliged to take on his friends in the debate, although he knew it would keep him longer with them than he wished. "Look chaps," he said. "It is this kind of statement Alinse is making, that encourages people to drink. There is also the talk that one can drink safely. It is all a guise to make money out of people's ignorance."

"Only the other day, I read about this claim in a local paper, where a journalist was writing about safe drinking, comparing it with safe sex. The message seems to be that you can do the wrong things safely," Alinse said.

"What kind of comparison is that, 'Drink safely' is as bad advice No matter how safely, which to some may mean taking a little drop each time. That pinch of spirit puts poison into your body slowly, until it begins to damage important organs of your body. They then stop functioning and you die. Now take sex. You take safety precautions, by avoiding intercourse with anyone suffering from one of those sexually transmitted diseases. Alternatively, you use condoms or any other barrier methods to protect you from contracting infection when having sex. If you do these things, you can go on having sex for as long as you have the sexual desire to do so. You do not die from having little or a lot of sex."

The issue was taking time to be resolved. Around their table guests were milling, some stopping to talk to Malu and his friends. Alinse was starting to speak, when a young man came over to greet him. He dismissed him quickly and then said "Malu, you miss the point. I still respect the advice of the experts. 'Control the amount you drink,' they say, and save yourself from premature death. Some experts actually specify the amount that is safe to drink. People who drink every day are advised to drink no more than three or four units of alcohol a day; for women two to three units."

"How does one know what measure is a unit?" Manga wanted to know.

"It is in most reputable wine dealers' shops," Alinse said. "But you can ask Radel. He is the medical doctor, but if my memory serves me well, if you have had a pint and a half of beer with 4% alcohol, you have had your safe ration for the day. For women, it's a small glass of wine"

"So, except for Mal, we've all had more than our full ration for the day," Manga said.

"So you see," Malu says with glee. "Alinse supports safe drinking and here he is practising the opposite."

"I don't drink every day, so the occasional excess doesn't count."

Malu seemed to have accepted his compulsory detention. He had no intention of staying long at the party, but wanted to avoid giving the impression that he was not one of their type.

"Hey!" his friends yelled. "Food service."

The waiters moved nearer to their table and served each of them an assortment of food in a large white square plate. All the delicacies of the season were assembled in the square, in a pattern defying the partaker to destroy the chef's art. In the middle of the plate was the food presented in the form of a flower. The sepals and petals were of green and red peppers stuffed with minced grouper. The stamens were slices of skinned cucumber stuck into moulded jollof rice, which formed the carpels. On opposite sides of the flower were two mid-cuts of grilled barracudas. As well as the main service, the waiters placed on the table side service of onion and pepper sauce, black eyed beans, and fried plantains.

"This is both beautiful and delicious," Manga spoke after digging into the body of the flower imitation and sampling its goodness. "It is sacrilege to destroy the art of the century. I plead guilty."

"I agree. This is classy. Trust Radel to go that extra mile to have the best for his guests," Malu said.

"You know, living so near to Yombo, has its advantages. Fresh fish is available every day," Manga said. "We Peninsula people live the longest in the country," he added with pride.

"You will be our Tithonus. He asked the gods to give him eternal life when he was old. You will stay like this forever, eating fresh fish daily, without appealing to the gods." Alinse said jokingly

"Alinse, don't you think Manga should be set daily fish consumption units, so he does not exceed the safe number of units that would guarantee his longevity?" Malu said.

"Surely, we could work something out," he said.

"Gentlemen, on that note, I must beg to leave." Malu rose and shook hands with his friends.

"Before you leave, Malu, I must introduce you to my young friend, Modu Kolen on the table here." Alinse pointed to the table where all the noise in the sitting room was coming from and then beckoned to his friend to come over.

"Koney," he said, "This is Dr. Modu Kolen. He studied History at Manola and Lagos." He only returned to the country last month and expects to join the staff of his Alma Mater in September." Malu extended a hand.

"Malu Koney" They shook hands. "Welcome back home. The field is wide open. There is much left to do, to properly record the history of our continent," he said.

"I am so glad to meet you sir," he replied. "I have heard so much about you and have read all your books. I certainly look forward to contributing my own small bit to that effort."

"Let's meet again under less suffocating circumstances," he said, handing him his business card.

He spun around to leave. Then, like an apparition, the girl in the church with the stunning looks, moved into the house from the garden where she had sat with other guests.

He stopped on seeing her. Modu Kolen was still standing near him. Both stood as the girl walked past. This time, he ignored her and walked away in a different direction from that which she was heading. It was Modu Kolen whose attention her sensuous figure gripped. It sparked in him the urge to approach her. He trailed her, brushing past one of his friends at his table. "I shall be back," he said, smiling. He soon caught up with her and delivered the most disingenuous tripe with practised charm. "Excuse me please. My name is Dr. Kolen," he said. "I notice you are one of the godparents. Where can I find Mrs. Lamara? I have a gift for the baby."

Kolen had earlier asked to see Mrs Lamara as soon as he entered the house. He had already handed over a present for her child and a cash contribution to the cost of the day's party. The deceit may have shown in his eyes, because she gave a mocking smile. She thought something may be sinister about this man who could fake ignorance so blatantly. However, she was thrilled that she could be sought after so desperately in that way. She decided to play along.

"I am," she said. "My name is Bina. "Mrs. Lamara is my aunt. I'll take you to her bedroom. She has gone upstairs to change the baby."

As they reached the first landing on the stairs, he stopped abruptly.

"Sorry lady," he said.

"I have seen her already. I only wanted to talk to you."

Modu's gaze was focused on her as he spoke. He was seeing the full face of the girl he followed to the stairs like a hound after its prey. Close up, she looked sexier than she did from a distance. Her face was more striking than the contour of the body that drove him to initiate the chase. It was oblong in a way that is unnoticeable; slightly wider at the level of the chin than at the temples. The brown colour that defined these features had shades of brownness across her cheeks, emphasizing a nose that rises inconspicuously from the well of the cheek bones. Her brown eyes were large, clear and bright; piercing and alluringly as Malu had found them.

She threw him a shyly but obstinate question. "About what?" she said.

"We can't stand here blocking the stairway talking about it?" He spoke hesitantly; he was edging out of control of his emotions.

"I hope it won't take long; I am with friends in the garden, who are waiting for me to return with a waiter to serve them more drinks."

"It won't take long, I assure you. We can move out to the front garden. It is quieter there."

Kolen looked down into the crowded ground floor and observed the movements of the guests. He weighed his chances of sneaking out with this young lady without being noticed, and decided the odds of that happening were good. He escorted her out of the house and into a part of the front garden where no one could see them from inside the house.

"I know that you will think me audacious to approach you unceremoniously like this, but I am that kind of person, hitting the iron while it is hot. I saw you first at the church, when you walked up with the child's parents to the front pew. Since I came with my friends to the house party, I had been hoping that I would bump into you and perhaps, introduce myself. So here I am."

"I am flattered," she said. "But how can you just burst into me from nowhere and expect me to rush into your arms like a long lost lover?"

"Far be it. I am only an enchanted bee who has seen a flower of exquisite beauty and is attempting to seek permission to hover around it."

"That's romantic; a poet, no doubt."

"No. I am a humble historian; and you?"

110

"I am at Teachers' College in Kosna. I finish next year, and will try to get into Nursing College after that."

Modu regretted opening their conversation into lengthy passage to his goal, but he carried on. "Why make a switch at so late in the course? Your parents would surely like you to start earning your living, having cost them three years of fees to get you that far."

"That does not worry them. They did not have to pay my fees, but they are quite supportive of my plans."

"I am making the change because I have found from my experience during my teaching practice, that I do not have the calling for that profession. I went into it because I was impressed by an appeal made to our final year class at school, that the country needed primary school teachers and that as many of us who would sign up for teaching would be awarded scholarships to train as professional teachers."

"How many of you who opted to train as teachers are now disillusioned about the profession?"

"I don't know. All I know is that some of my schoolmates who went into nursing are enjoying their training."

"There is no guarantee that you will find it as enjoyable as they have found it."

"I am sure I will.

Bina seemed comfortable with her decision to make a change of professional interest. She was among many young girls in the country, who entertained negative views of the teaching profession. They were convinced that the profession was not as rewarding as it used to be.

To them, nursing was different. Many of Bina's friends, who were graduating from Nursing College, loved the courses.

"I admire your confidence," Modu said.

"I have carefully considered the pros and cons of this change to nursing. It is a profession that elevates practitioners to the level of goddesses. Like notional goddesses, they dispense care through spiritual guidance. The treatment and medication that they administer, are the physical application of the results of medical research; but what promotes the effectiveness of the applications, was the transfer from nurse to patient of the power of unquestionable conviction, that the applications will result in a cure."

"That is impressive. I respect that analysis in the context of altruism. We are all placed in this world to save humanity using our God-given gifts. I have chosen to work in higher education, hoping to direct young students' minds to pursue knowledge in the direction in which their intellect would lead them. My teacher at Makoron Secondary School always quoted lines from the English poet, Tennyson. One of the ones I remember is:

"...... this Grey spirit yearning in desire
To follow knowledge like a sinking star,
Beyond the utmost bound of human thought."

"I remember that line too. It is from Ulysses. It was one of the set poems for our National School Leaving Examination's English Literature examination paper. Our teacher told us that it is based on a Greek character.

It portrays Ulysses as one who continually strove without relenting, to reach beyond the limits of possibility."

"I am no Greek, but that quotation should be an inspiration for all who wish to explore knowledge with determination, until they succeed. I am happy that I met you at last. I have thoroughly enjoyed our conversation. Now I would like to meet you again, introduce you to my friends and take you out for a meal somewhere in the city."

"There is a problem with that. You see, there is a guy on the table where I am sitting with my friends. He has done nothing else since the service was over, but tried to be friendly. His persistence has won him a date. I quite like you. You are forthright and quite entertaining to talk to, but I cannot promise anything."

"You are not yet married to him. Are you?"

"No. That would have been a world record for a couple getting married on the first day they met. However, it is not my habit to be seeing two blokes at the same time. Girls in my dormitory manage it, I can't."

"That is a point to consider. I respect that."

"Here is a compromise. Give me your card and if things turn out differently, I'll call you."

"Your honesty baffles me, but I accept."

He searched his inside pocket, extracted a visiting card, and wrote:

"This is to a friend to whom I'd like to give my heart."

He handed it to her.

Surprised and flattered by the inscription, she moved towards him and kissed him on the cheeks.

"Remember your promise to me on the stairway, 'It won't take long?' Here is mine. 'It may not be too long.'" Then she ran off to the front door and disappeared into the house.

Having chosen to avoid meeting the girl who earlier mesmerized him, Malu reached the end of the set of tables at the rear end of the room and searched for a passage to the front entrance. There at a table before him were his aunts. He could not avoid them not seeing him. He went to join them and said:

"I am on my way out."

"That's early," Aunt Macile said." "Radel would not like you leaving so early. You have been close friends since childhood. I do not see him taking it kindly if you were to leave before the end of the party."

"I've left Cecala at home with Mark and Abi. She is pregnant again and has been unwell this last week. Of late, she has been seeing her doctor frequently for problems connected with this pregnancy. Besides, our house help does not work on Sundays, so I ought to get back as soon as possible. I have also promised to see my Papa before I return to Clendon."

"All right then, but you do not seem your usual buoyant self today. It shows in your face. Even in church, you looked distracted to the extent that I had to nudge you several times to get your attention back to the service. You cannot tell us it is all due to worries about Cecala?"

"Certainly, there are other worries, including the uncertainties of life at the present time."

"We are feeling it too, Malu," Aunty Bani commented. "Just keep focussed on what you do, despite the rumblings around you," she advised.

"Look at us, we manage despite all the problems we face. Look at the economic situation, for example. The cost of living is spiralling out of control, throwing more people into an abyss of utter deprivation. The town's population has exploded. You see the result of this in crowds milling around in the streets, many aimlessly and without jobs." Aunt Macile joined in and spoke agitatedly.

A young girl brought some drinks for the ladies and served them out. When she left, Aunty Banie turned to Malu and said "Your aunt is always excited about issues she feels concerned about. There has always been movement into this area from the interior, but since the incursion of rebels across one of our border towns, we have seen a huge influx of people from affected areas seeking safety in the town. This problem is bound to affect the nation economically and socially. One has to leave it to the government to handle that."

"True, that is why we have a government to deal with emergencies like this and help displaced people settle into safe areas and given the means to live as normal a life as possible. They should not have to be left to their own devices, to fend for themselves," Aunt Macile countered.

"Something is being done, Macile. The young officers who run the country now are doing their best, and are popular."

"Popular with young people only, I dare say," Aunty Macile said. "It is a craze. They see themselves as part of the ruling machine," she continued.

"It boosts their ego; some of them have formed groups to keep the town clean, all on their own volition," Aunty Banie said.

"That may be so, but feeling part of the ruling machine has gained them nothing. They form the bulk of the jobless in the town. That is why we have so much burglary now. Slum dwellings are being erected in rapid succession in and around Bonor Warf. The displaced in the town have no decent place to live. Squalor breeds crime and disease. We shall all have to face the consequences of this overcrowding someday," Aunty Macile said.

Macile saw from the corner of her eyes, a man on the table nearest to theirs looking at her as she spoke. Always the contentious type, she said to Malu, "Do you know that man over there looking straight at me?" "That is Dr. Lamara's brother, Kella. He is a teacher at the Munga Secondary School. I don't think he means harm. I'll call him over. He beckoned to him. He came over and greeted the ladies.

"You were eavesdropping on us. What's your interest?" Aunty Macile questioned, being her direct self.

"Nothing really. I heard you talking about the squalor in the town. That caught my attention, because it is the very issue we were discussing on our table," he said.

"Then none of us can do anything about it. But worse, is the way the roads have become impassable and drainage channels used as garbage dumps," Macile said.

"The local council has the responsibility to clear these regularly, to prevent flooding during the rainy season," Kella remarked.

Banie then said, "It is nice to talk. Let me ask you; with what money, shall the council do this. They receive their funds from the central government. How can the council get money from the central government, when the country is fighting insurgents at the country's boarder?"

"The border problems started four years ago, Banie. We have had this problem for so long and nothing has ever been done." Macile was on her hobby horse again. Kella smiled, then said, "We have to get you elected into parliament when we are allowed to vote again" and returned to his table.

When Kella left, Macile continued with her attack on the management of the affairs of the country. "This is what I will like to know from all of you. 'Where have all the taxes we paid from our salaries, over the thirty years we slaved away teaching the nation's children, gone?'"

"You'll have to ask that of the deposed President," Banie said.

"The squalor we see around is part of the indiscipline of the present generation. It all boils down to declining standards in every sphere of our lives. Our people too have played a part in all of that," Macile said.

"I think we teachers must feel that the effort we made teaching those kids was wasted. I think we should feel sad, looking at how the new generation children have turned out; lawless, disrespectful, money hungry and wanting what they cannot afford," Banie added.

Malu had been left out of the conversation so far. It served his purpose, but then he could not help throwing in a comment to humour them.

"Don't complain," he said. "You failed to teach those sound morals of uprightness and truthfulness. That is why many of the children have turned out the way they are today."

"Come on, Malu, we did our best. After all, in our time, we had them for only six hours a day and five days a week. Today, the present teachers have them for less time than we had. Their parents have them for the larger part of the day. They have them at weekends and throughout the holidays. Given that they have more time with their kids than teachers have, they carry the greater responsibility to train them to be good citizens."

"Well said," Malu spoke courteously, and rising from his seat, continued, "I've had enough social awareness briefing for the day, ladies. I must run off to see Papa before returning to Clendon."

Chapter 12

Madika and Rose Koney woke up that Sunday morning healthy looking. They looked forward to attending the 10.30 a.m. church service. There were three services on Sundays, 8.30 a.m., 10.30 a.m. and 12.00 noon. They preferred the 10.30 a.m. service, because it gave Madika more time to lie in. Since his illness, a year earlier, he had been going to bed at 7 p.m. and getting up late in the morning. He had also given up working in the garden. Rose had continued with some crop production on the plot for another year when she felt she could no longer continue with Madika needing more of her attention. They had rented the plot to a neighbour and kept control of the chicken coop and tool shed on it.

Madika's daily departure to bed early, made Rose furious in the beginning. "You are behaving like a sick cockerel," she often teased him. Once he had gone to bed, she had no company, so she had learnt to make necklaces and mats with beads. Luckily, her products attracted great interest when she first displayed them at the quarterly bring and buy sale of her church. Since then, her bead-work had become sought-after items at these sales. With a guaranteed outlet for what she made, she worked contented in the loneliness of her evenings. She regarded them as time spent in the service of God and with profitable returns being only incidental. The mornings were different. She had her standard early morning routine which she set into motion as soon as she got out of bed. She would first let out the chickens and see that the tenant who now worked their back-yard plot was settled in the compound. She would then go into the kitchen, light the small kerosene stove and boil enough water in their large whistling kettle, to fill their thermos flask. She would put it in the middle of the dining table and proceed to set three places for breakfast; three plates, three cups, spoons fork and knives. They had kept the table arrangement since their son Malu returned from university and was teaching at the Peninsula Secondary School. He had told his mother that he would like to join them at meal times at table laid out as was done at his university hall of residence. He hated being served separately in a bowl, as her Mum did when he was younger. The bowl was left in the kitchen table, so he could help himself as and when he wanted to. They had continued with the three-place arrangement even after Malu left home for studies overseas. Madiku had said then, "Let's keep the extra place, Rose, so we are always ready to share a meal with any stranger who turns up." Satisfied with the setting, she would sit on a chair by a front window and read her bible until her husband was out of bed, when she joined him for morning prayers.

On the Sunday of the christening of the Lamara's daughter, it was Madika and Rose's turn to man the church entrance and welcome worshipers to the 10.30 a.m. service. They had to be at church earlier than usual, so they held only brief prayers and left to perform their Sunday duty. After returning home from church, they changed into their house clothes and went out to the back porch. There were six cane chairs lined on the paved area, two of them with foot rests. Madika loved sitting where he could face the garden. For most people in the town, Sunday was the day for visiting friends and relatives. Madika and Rose had done enough of visiting in their time. They had stopped the practice. But when Malu or his wife felt they should visit family or friends together on important occasions, they would arrange to take them out and bring them back home. The Sunday afternoon started out quietly. They sat on the chairs that had foot rests and read passages of scripture to each other. They stopped reading when Madika stumbled on a word that triggered the recall of an episode in his life that occurred years before he met Rose. He did not say what it was. He just stopped in the middle of the passage and put down his bible. They both sat still for a while, looking out into the rows of well laid out vegetable plants, stretching back to the boundary of their property. At the odd moment, Madika would say, "God be praised." Rose would say, "Amen."

Nearing mid-day, Rose went back into the house to prepare a light mid-day meal. They ate their main meals in the evenings, a practice from the days they worked long hours on their Duru farm which they still continued. When the meal was ready, she brought it out to the porch where they ate and chatted happily between mouthfuls. Madika was dozing off after the meal, when two friends of theirs from the neighbourhood arrived with their three children. They came through the yard gate as they often did; easier to meet them where they normally spent the day. They were members of the same bible study group at Okeju Evangelical, as Madika and Rose.

They joined the church six months earlier. They were newcomers, who had arrived from Fadiba, a town close to the country's border area where there had been fighting. On their baptism and confirmation as members of the church, the pastor had assigned them to Madika's group. They met for Bible study every week on Thursdays at members' houses in rotation. The two families had developed close friendship over the months that they had been interacting at the Thursday meetings.

"Blessing to this house," they said, announcing their arrival. Madika propped himself up from his reclining posture, "Welcome brother and sister. I did not see much of you people in church today and you were absent from the church group meeting last Thursday at the Wildor's." Half conscious, he managed to spit the words out.

They explained that that they were out of town at a wedding engagement at their home town, where the bride-to-be came from. They explained that in a small town like Fadiba, everyone was related. It would have been a crime for them to miss such an occasion. They were surprised that the Waldors did not give their apologies, since they had sent one through them.

Apparently restored fully to consciousness, Madika ventured a suggestion as the children moved into his view. "Get yourselves some place to sit," he said. "Good afternoon Sir, good afternoon, Ma." The children rolled the words out of their tongues like a song. "How are you all?" Madika spoke normally, having recovered from his drowsiness.

"How are you doing at school?"

"We are doing well, Sir," again they gave it to him, sing-song like, in unison.

"That's how you must keep it children. Keep doing well. Without education, you can't make a decent life for yourself and your family, if you eventually have one."

He had given this advice so many times before to young people. He often wondered whether it had done much to inspire them.

Rose got up from her chair and went into the kitchen. She returned with a tray of food she had prepared hurriedly and some drinks. On the tray were bottles of ginger beer, *akara balls* and ground nut cakes. She served the visitors and returned the tray to the kitchen. She came back and sat with them. They spoke about church matters; how their church was expanding and building up a large reserve fund. There were now 500 members, up by 150 since last Christmas. Under their Pastor Elijah, the church had brought Christ to many in and around Munga. Madika believed Pastor Elijah could carry out miracles.

"I have seen how the pastor uses his name to heal the sick and drive out evil spirit from confessed witches," he said.

"You should see how they shudder and scream when the devil leaves them," Rose added.

Their visitors agreed that they had heard of those miracles being performed and would like to see such wonders. They expressed the wish to attend the next revival when it was organized, so that they could request special prayers for relief of their desperate condition. Madika and Rose had supported their family with food, old clothes and money, when they first arrived in Munga. They had always been grateful to them for the love they had showed their family. They knew that coming to a busy town like Munga, without a lot of money, was almost like jumping from a sinking boat without a life vest. In many cases, life sometimes forces one to jump if one had to, hoping for a miracle rescue.

Madika spoke about progress in the church and encouraged them to have hope that their condition would change for the better. "Whatever you ask for through fasting and prayers, God always answers, so long as you are sincere in your prayers," Madika told them. He went on to say that he and Rose had been at fasting and prayer sessions for about two weeks now, asking God to give their son success in his bid to win an important position at his institute. Pastor Elijah had been leading the prayers. He said that they had felt the uplifting spirit of those prayers and were certain of a successful answer to their prayers

As the adults were engrossed in conversation, the children made themselves scarce. They slipped away into the garden. They soon found themselves at Rose's chicken coop. They stood by the wire cage and fed the chickens with pieces of the ground nut cake Rose had served them. Afterwards, they moved from the chickens and walked to the back of the yard. There they found a hammock fitted between two mango tree branches. That was where they were, taking turns swinging merrily back and forth, when their parents called out to them.

"Come on children it's time to go home. There's school tomorrow. You have to prepare your school work while it is still daylight."

They ran to the porch and joined their parents. They said their goodbyes and left.

When they left, Rose went to the chicken coop and drove the chickens from the outer wire cage into the wooden shelter. She then transferred the feeding bowls and water troughs to the shelter and locked the chickens for the night. Madika was sitting in his favourite chair in the sitting room, when Rose walked in. She found him sitting in a lounging position with his eyes focused on the blank white ceiling. He had the appearance of a man in deep thoughts. His lips were pressed firmly together, bringing up his cheeks into a mild frown. His hair had receded slightly from the forehead, but had only a few grey strands, fewer than you would expect on the head of a man his age. Rose collected her work basket from the cupboard on the wall of the dining room and took them to her rocking chair. She turned on the radio, found the gospel music station, and leaned back, her hands expertly stringing her beads. She had to prepare the evening meal, but it was too early for that. Rose had a surprise planned for dinner. Madika loved cat fish cooked in groundnut oil and seasoned with *patmangie,* herbs. She had secured some of the herbs from the tenant farming the back garden. Madika did not eat meats of any kind any more. Not so much because of his food restrictions after his last illness, but because meat fibres usually stuck between what was left of his molars and they were painful to remove. He was no fan of afters, either. To eat anything sweet or not after a delicious main dish was an abomination to him. "It spoils the taste of the meal," he often said. He wanted the aroma of the food he had eaten, to linger in his mouth as long as it lasted. This was the way he thought he could appreciate the goodness of God, who had given him the appetite to enjoy what he has had made for our sustenance.

While Rose was working on her beads, he could hear the slow low-pitched grunts of her husband as if coming from afar. That alarmed her, knowing that if he fell asleep on his chair, nothing less than an electric shock would stir him to life. Besides, he had to be fed well before his bedtime, which was getting close. "Madika! Dinner will soon be ready. Don't you ever attempt to fall asleep at this time of the day," she shouted. Without waiting to confirm that he heard her, she went into the kitchen to prepare her husband's favourite dish. They were expecting Malu to visit them that evening. He had sent word that he would call in to see them after attending the christening ceremony of the daughter of his friend Radel. Rose hoped that he could join them for dinner before returning home. So, she set a place for him on the dining table. When the food was ready, and there was no sign of Malu, Rose called Madika to the table. He was surprisingly alert. When Rose told him that she had prepared his favourite dish for dinner, the appreciation showed immediately in the grin on his face. They ate in a cheerful atmosphere.

After dinner, Madika left the table and returned to his seat by the window. Rose put the dishes away, reserving some of the remaining food for Malu, in case he wanted to eat when he arrived. She went back to her rocking chair, and in contented mood rocked herself to the rhythm of the gospel music rising from the little chrome-lined radio box on the stand beside her chair.

A Future Imperfect/Kosonike Koso-Thomas

Chapter 13

Malu left his friend's house after spending more time at his child's christening party than he had planned. He wanted to talk to his father about the turn of events at Kilinde. The drive from Radel's house to his father's, took only ten minutes. From where he sat, Madika had seen his son approaching the house. Just as he was about to knock on the front door, he turned the door knob and opened it. Malu walked into the sitting room in front of him. "Good afternoon Papa," he said. His father closed the door behind him. He heard the sound of choral music floating softly through the air. He traced its source to the small radio on the wooden stand by a rocking chair. His mother sat, dreamily rocking and humming the tune in the air, while threading beads through a length of raffia strands. .

Malu walked over and greeted his Mum. Moving away from her to grab a seat, he said, "I've been at the christening of Jame's daughter. Aunt Macile and Aunty Banie were there. They send their greetings." The old man took a seat next to his son, who saw his father's eyes glittering with excitement. "It must be good news about the Institute's President job." His thoughts went back to the last time Malu visited them, two weeks after his interview. He hinted then that an announcement of the successful contender was likely to be made two weeks later. "That should be about now," his father said, reminding him that it was about time for an announcement to be made. Seeing his father's anxiety

Malu decided not to break the disappointing news to his Papa until he had allowed his anxiety to cool. He was his father's favourite son. His elder brother had not made much of his life. Since he left home, at the age of nineteen, to work in the diamond mines in the east, his family had not heard from him. Malu was his parent's only source of support in their old age. His father adored him. He followed his progress keenly, rejoicing at his successes and brooding over his setbacks, which were hardly serious. Malu considered how he could devise a soft landing for the disappointing news he had come to deliver. He decided to start with news about the new government decrees expected to be announced soon. He said, "I have inside information that bus fares are to be regulated by government. Some fares may even come down by forty percent."

The subject of rising fares to and out of Munga was one about which his father had strong views. "I am glad to hear that; travel cost has been so high recently, that it has become too expensive for most people. Travelling to the city for my eye checks at the Pennson Hospital now costs twice as much as they did six months ago," his father said

"I am glad too," his mother looked up from her beads and added in a low even voice, "bus operators charge according to the number of people in the queue. They know that there is serious shortage of buses in our area and that people are desperate to travel, whatever the cost. Market women are the most exploited of the lot. Because they can get better prices for their goods in the city, they risk their lives, travelling with their wares in trucks and open vans, most of them too dangerous to be on the roads." Hearing his mother speak, he looked towards her. She was the calm one, not readily showing her emotions. He knew that she would understand what he was about to disclose to them. She was a down-to-earth person. Unlike his Papa, she had never held as high an expectation of her son, as his father did. Malu thought back to the time when he came home and told his parents he had passed his Common Entrance Examination. All his mother said, was, "My boy, so long as you passed your examination, I am happy." He looked away from his mother and met his father's gaze. His eyes were focused on him as if taking in every minute detail of the image of the son he so loved, and of whom he was infinitely proud. He was not certain that it was time to reveal the reason for his visit. He thought he needed to stretch the settling time further, so he said, "How is your tenant doing with the farming at the back garden so far? She seems determined to have taken off nicely from you folk."

"Yes, she is doing well," his mother said. "You know; it was at church that we were introduced to her and her parents."

Judging the climate perfect for his bombshell, he stood up from the chair on which he sat, moved closer to his father, and touched him on his shoulder.

"Papa," he said at last, "I lost the job of President of the institute. I think I shall have to leave the institute," his voice trailing off into a whisper. His father pushed him aside and shouted, "Rose, did you hear that?" He rose from his chair screaming. It was so loud; the neighbours could hear the crackling sound of distress if not the words it carried. "How can it be that on this God's own day, the fading sun will cause shadows of shame and distress to fall upon this humble home," he said.

"Papa," she called him Papa, the title her children used. "To God we must leave our disappointment," she said. "He knows best and he will make it plain to us later."

"Why have we not seen this coming in our prayer sessions at church or here at home?"

"That question is not for us to answer. Other things were revealed to us. We thank God for it." She turned off the radio, put her beads away and rose from her rocking chair. With slow halting steps, she walked towards Malu and hugged him tenderly saying, "I have seen the signs; a greater honour awaits you. It will be a perfect future."

"Thank you, Mama, I know you mean well for me."

His father stared at his wife as if transfixed by the news. Then he moved slowly and unsteadily to the sofa against the wall in front of him. He sat with his two hands on his legs. He was breathing heavily, his head bowed. "Whom did they give it to?" he enquired. There was sadness in his eyes. The anticipation of success for his son had been inflated to such a high pressure, that reality of failure simply shattered every belief that sustained it.

"You don't need to know Papa. He is not from anywhere you know."

"Just curious who the lucky winner was, because, none can be more deserving than you."

"Salac Fanda. The council favoured him because the majority of members felt that he would suit their mollifying stance with government. I was too much a man who sticks to his guns, the council feared."

"Salac Fanda." His father spoke the name with the fury of a man presented with the bill for drinks he didn't order. "No! They cheated you out of it. The rumour we heard from the campus was that you were the front runner. How can the situation change so dramatically?" He raised his hands to his head and clutched them across the top of his skull. "Cheating is stealing. It says in the bible 'Thou shalt not steal; thou shalt not bear false witness against thy neighbour.' There is too much of the violations of the Ten Commandments handed down to Moses on Mount Sinai. Our pastor at church has always preached that deliverance from sin and death, comes from obedience to the teachings of Christ and his disciples."

His father's speech was hardly audible. It seemed as if the words were filtered through a sound box that was faulty. He dropped his hands to his side and slowly brought his body to a reclining position on the sofa. He had suffered a stroke, the second in the year.

His father's face looked strained; his hands were now folded across his chest. He was breathing heavily. He made an attempt to sit upright on the sofa and couldn't. Malu noticed that he was restless and inconvenient. He rushed to his parent's bedroom and brought out a pillow. He grabbed him under the arms and put his back against an arm of the sofa, then slipped the pillow under his head. He made for the kitchen and returned with a cup of water.

"Here Papa, you look dazed and weak." His father took a sip from the cup and fell back to rest his head on the pillow.

Malu became extremely worried about his father's condition. "Mama, I am not happy with the way Papa looks," he said to his mother. His father interrupted him. "I am fine," he said. Then slurring, he continued. "Just a bit weak, that's all. It will pass." He had experienced the same weakness the Saturday before, at Okeju Evangelical, when he had attended a special fasting and prayer session for the deliverance of Malu from enemies around him. Before Malu's interview, he had told the pastor that people wanted to deny his son success at his interview for the President's position. That prayer session was supposed to cancel the effect of all evil manipulations against his son. It had been a long session, with repeated standing and kneeling. Madika felt week and dizzy. He slumped on to the edge of his pew, gasping for breath. Everything seemed to be spinning around him. He had to hold on to the chair next to him to stop him falling to the ground.

"At our prayer meeting last week, I had the same experience, but it passed off quickly."
"Papa, episodes like these should not be taken lightly. I am going to call Radel to examine you and see that there is no gathering health storm which needed lifting, before it became dangerous."
"I told you, I'm fine, there is nothing wrong with me, only a slight upset at the news of your failure to win the job."

"You definitely don't look well."

Malu turned to his mother, obviously concerned. He spoke with a firm voice.

"Mama, Papa is sick. He is weak and confused."

"What are you saying son?"

"Papa needs medical attention, immediately and I am going to call my friend Radel to come over and see him."

"With all those guests in his house, will he be able to come?"

"He is his doctor. He has been looking after him since his heart attack last year. He knows Pa's case. He will be most willing to answer an emergency call from us. Besides, he is like a brother; you know that, don't you? He will turn up, Mama."

His mother moved to the sofa and sat beside her husband, holding his hand and rubbing it. Turning to Malu she said, "You are a doctor. Let Radel have this important day with his family. Do what you can."

"Mama, I am not that type of doctor. I don't cure illnesses; I try to cure ignorance in people with the books I write."

Rose moved to the top end of the sofa and touched her husband's brows. "You will be all right, Madika," she said.

"Mama, can you help me to take Papa to his bed? He couldn't get there on his own."

He and his mother got him on to his feet. Arm in arm they walked him to his bed. He laid silently on his back, looking at the ceiling with glazed eyes. His wife sat by his side while Malu called Radel on his mobile phone. As soon as he had finished talking to his friend, he called Cecala, his wife and told her that his father had taken ill suddenly. He told her that the crisis would delay his return home.

"I want to see him in stable condition before I leave," he said.

"Is it that serious?" Cecala asked.

"Nothing I hope Radel can't handle, but I will explain on my return.

Radel received the call while photographs were being taken of the newly baptized child and her parents. Receiving emergency calls on Sundays ruined his day. Happening on a day when his family was celebrating a special event of a kind that hardly occurred every year, any call would be considered an unpardonable intrusion. But Malu was his close personal friend. Radel regarded Malu's father as his own father. He therefore regarded it a duty to attend to that emergency. He called his wife aside and told her of the emergency. He then rushed out of his house with his medical bag and emergency kit. He was at Malu's house in less than ten minutes. Malu led him to the room where his father lay and watched him from the foot of the bed with folded arms, as he carried out his examination. His mother left the room and waited in the sitting room for a verdict.

"Tell me how you feel Pa?" the doctor asked.

"I'm OK now that I am lying down. Earlier, I was weak and dizzy and felt a sharp pain running down my left hand like an electric shock."

"Pa, have you been taking your medicines? You should not be panting like this if you kept to the regime I put you on a month ago."

"To tell the truth, Radel, I stopped taking them two weeks ago when we started our weekly fasting and prayers at the church. Our pastor told us that we should deny ourselves everything that goes into our stomachs, till we receive the revelation that our prayers have been answered."

"Pa, you must learn to listen more to your doctor when it comes to advice about your health, not your pastor." Turning to Malu, he said,

"We need to arrange for one of my nurses to come in every day to administer his medicines, once we get over this crisis."

The doctor opened his bag and took out his stethoscope, blood pressure machine and other tubes and syringes. He quickly went through multiple steps, physically examining him. That completed, he took his blood pressure to complete his examination. At the end of it, he pulled Malu aside and said, "We've just escaped a major catastrophe. I'll give him some new tablets to stabilize him during the night. Bring him a glass of water and let's see that he takes them right now."

I'll arrange for him to be taken for an angiogram at Pennson Hospital in the morning."

Malu walked his friend to the door. He had to deal with an unexpected disaster that had shattered the usual calm of his weekends. He opened the door to let his friend out, but his mind was in another place, wondering whether he had caused this latest medical incident that may rob his dad of the life he had left. He quickly wiped it off his mind.

Suddenly, he felt a tap on his back, bringing him back to the present. It was from Radel. "Mal, how did the headship contest go?"

He did not hear at first. His friend repeated the question. "It went to Salac Fanda," Malu said. "I believe that the choice was made for convenience. The Governing Council wanted a President it could work with comfortably."

"What do you mean by comfortably?"

"Having to tell the head of the institute what to do and it gets done without any argument. That's now done. However, I don't see me working under him. I'll have to leave."

"I cannot believe that the outcome would turn out so badly for you. But you don't have to leave the Institute now. I hear that you are the most respected academic on the campus. President or no President, the staff will look up to you. The world knows you through your books."

"That counts for little Radel. I will always be subject to the authority of the President of the Institute. The fact that I was his rival for the position, puts him in a defensive position every time I chance to express a view other than his."

"Why? You are a man of your own mind. Your views will be heard and will count for much in the institute."

"That's the worry. If I stayed, Falac will be looking over his shoulders expecting sabotage from me."

"You could continue with your research, write your books and keep away from him."

"It is easier said than done Radel. I am a member of the Academic Board. I just can't go to meetings, sit there like a dumb bird, and walk out again, fearing that some of what I will say may be interpreted as criticism of the boss. My best option is to leave."

Radel was seemingly upset. He said with an unusually low voice, "as for Pa, I will follow his treatment through. You get back to Cecala. I will be here in the morning to supervise Dad's transfer to Pennson."

"Thanks, Radel. Kindly tell my aunts, Banie and Macile that their brother has fallen ill."

"Thanks for nothing, Mal. You can't imagine how much trouble we doctors have with some of these pastors of fortune. They amass wealth through donations from their congregations, whom they entice with prophesies and promises of cure for all types of diseases. All over the country, these pastors and their churches are mushrooming. Not long ago, doctors used to warn patients about seeking treatment from Juju medicine men, who claim to have powers to cure even the deadliest disease. Now we have the pastors to contend with."

"My dear Radel, everybody is referring to what we have today as the free society. There is no seeming control over anything. We are at the mercy of unscrupulous people, who defy authority and challenge the social order. Nothing assures us that after these pastors have finished doing their worst, there won't be other miracle healers taking their place, claiming powers greater than today's miracle men. The people can only be on their guard against their influences."

Radel said goodbye. He had work of a different kind waiting for him at home. Malu went back into the bedroom. His father lay still, but in a stable condition as expected after the sedation the doctor had administered. His eyes were open, but they showed signs of drowsiness. He took his father's left hand into his right and held it. He was furious at his dad's carelessness over his health, but knew that he should not excite him in any way. He caressed the hand and for a few moments kept his gaze on him until he caught his eyes. Then he spoke calmly.

"Papa," he said, you ought to remember the anxious time you gave us a year ago. You nearly died. You should not risk your life again by following questionable advice from people who are not qualified doctors."
"I am sorry son; Pastor Elijah is a good man of God, who performs miracles. I went into fasting and praying just for you. Yes, I did it for you, and will do it again so you can have the best that God has ordained for you."
"Well, it is kind of you to have my interest at heart, but see how far that has taken you with Pastor Elijah. And for the success for which you fasted and prayed, you know now the outcome. You must stop worrying about me. Have a good night's sleep and I will see you tomorrow at Pennson Hospital. Radel is arranging for you to be taken there for further examination and tests."

He left the bedroom and searched for his mother. He found her in the kitchen serving out some food. "You need to have something in your stomach before you leave."   "Mama, I won't be needing anything more today after the sumptuous meal I had at Radel's. Just see that Papa sleeps without disturbance. Radel will be here in the morning with a nurse, to give him his medicine. After that he will be taken to Pennson Hospital for tests."

"Is he going to get well soon?"

"By God's grace. I am sure everything will be done for him, to get him back to good health. Anyway Mama, I want to know why you allowed Papa to stop taking his medication when the doctor had told you to see that he takes them daily. It is late now. I'll leave that for tomorrow. I must go."

Chapter 14

As soon as his aunts learnt from Radel that their brother had taken ill, they left the christening party and hurried to his house. They were lucky to get a taxi to take them to their brother's house within minutes of them walking out of Radel's house into the street.

"Why did Malu have to send Radel to tell us of Madika's illness? What pride? He could not even call us himself," Macile said as they alighted from the taxi. The two sisters had gone through their earlier years as friends, although Macile was older. They often saw themselves as more enlightened than their brother, since they were better educated. When they were school-going girls, they spent all their holidays at home with their parents in Numbaya. While on holiday, they read and discussed books they were reading, sometimes in the presence of their brother, who thought they were deliberately showing off their knowledge. On one occasion, they attempted to call his attention to the lack of clarity in his speech, when he spoke to the minister after a church service. They had just taken their turn to speak to the minister who had asked them how they were spending their holidays, when Madika moved up to join them. The minister asked him about his interests. Madika did not speak clearly, so the poor Englishman had to ask him more than once, to repeat his statement. "Could you repeat that?" He kept on asking, until he gave up. "That's good," he said at last. His sisters knew that the minister was being diplomatic, not willing to embarrass the boy any further. When they reached home, the girls kept taunting him about his bad English, until he stormed off to the back yard where his father was sitting. He reported them to him, vowing that he would never speak to them again. Their father calmed him down with some fitting words, then went into the house and strongly reprimanded the girls. He told them that fluency in English did not make them more intelligent than their brother.

"Madika is brighter than you both," their father said. "Its only that he has not had the opportunity to get the kind of education you girls were having. In time, that will happen."

In later years, Banie blossomed into a lady, careful with her diet and her looks. She would spend hours deciding which clothes to wear and which shoes would match them. She would plait her hair so that it fell on the sides of her face, to draw attention to the dimples on her cheeks. Macile was a different kind of girl. She would speak her mind, regardless of the company she was in. She was often rough and brash, to the embarrassment of Banie. She would tell her sister that she was too conscious of her good looks; that she painted herself up like a doll for sale at an auction. Although Banie had many male admirers, it seemed that none of them was good enough for her. Macile had always told her that she was too choosy and that she might one day end up a spinster. That prediction came to pass. It was Macile who got married at 27. Banie, at 73 was still unmarried.

It was getting dark when Banie and Macile left the Lamara's house, but they considered it best to see their

brother right away, rather than wait till the morning. They were at the door of the Madika's five minutes after they alighted from the taxi. They knocked on the door. The force of the blows almost pulled it off its hinges. They may not have seen the door bell, but their anxiety to see their sick brother and the fact that neither Rose nor her son had taken the trouble to call them individually about the illness, had angered them and they were hunting for a fight. Rose heard the noise from the kitchen. She hurried to a front window and parted the curtains slightly, then looked out towards the door. Before she could make out any form at the door, another battering jolted her. She moved back from the window. She thought of calling the police, when she heard the voices of the ladies announcing their arrival. "Rose, it is Macile. I am with Banie. Please open the door, we are not robbers."
"Wait a minute, I'll get the key. We don't leave the key in the lock at night."

Rose found the keys and opened the door. They marched in like commandos on a search and kill mission. There were no greetings, no suppressed emotions. They went straight to the point.
"Where is Madika? O my God, what is happening to him? We want to see him." Macile was speaking and pacing up and down the room." Rose quickly realized that these women were going to cause trouble. She prepared herself mentally to deal with what was coming.

"Rose, when did this happen? Can we see him?" Banie asked with a restrained, but clearly concerned voice.

"He is sleeping now. The doctor said that he should not be disturbed and I should see that he gets a good night's sleep."

"So, we his sisters cannot even look at his ailing face and pray for him?"

"I don't know about that."

"I know. You just try us and see. We are going to see him, whether you like it or not." Macile shouted. She seemed agitated. "We have rights here, you know. This is our brother's house. We will do what we feel is our right."

The line between sister and wife was getting blurred. Blood rights now seem to be pitched against marital rights.

"This is my house too. I am in charge here." She stood in front of them, barring them from going past her into the corridor that led to the bedrooms.

"You are mistaken. This is Munga, not Sambu, where being a chief's daughter counts for something."

"I am only telling you what the doctor has ordered me to do. I will carry it out fully. It is in the interest of your brother's health. The doctor will be here in the morning and he will be mad at me for not following his instruction, if something goes wrong."

"Well here is our instruction," Macile said. "You take us to see our brother, or we shall force you out of our way and enter his bedroom."

Rose chose to lower the temperature of the exchanges. She spoke in a compromising tone.

"I beg you in God's name Macile; let us not quarrel over such a simple matter and make matters worse. Madika is ill. In the state in which you are right now, there is the risk that you will be unable to control your emotions and upset him. That will certainly set back his recovery."

"Macile, Rose is right. Only the doctor knows how delicate Madika's condition is and how to deal with it. Let us respect that."

"Banie, you are always the soft one. I know this woman. She is an idiot. She is not capable of looking after our brother."

"You can talk. How about you? Were you capable of looking after your own husband? You molested the poor man until it became for him, a matter of staying with you and be killed or leaving and live. He wisely chose the latter."

"Do you know whom you are talking to? Repeat that slander again, I shall wring your neck, and nothing will come of it."

"Macile, this is not the time to pick a quarrel with Rose. She has enough on her hands."

"You may say what you like. She has been offensive and awful. I'll teach her a lesson some other time when we are through with this worrying situation."

Rose walked to the door of the bedroom. The key was in the lock on the other side of the door. She quietly turned the door handle and removed the key. She then pulled the door gently and locked it. She removed the key, walked a few paces, and then turned to face the two sisters.

"Let me see how you get in there, Miss Macile," she said and walked past them into the kitchen.

They stood looking at each other in amazement. After about five minutes of silence, they decided to leave.

It took Malu two hours to reach home. He went back the way he came. Luckily for him there was no serious traffic jam at Malaba town. Cecala was expecting him to arrive much later than he did, having heard from him that his father had taken ill again and that he would be back late having to ensure that the old man got adequate medical care before leaving.

"Welcome," she said, as he entered his home. "How is the patient's condition now?" Cecela spoke with concern, but with some liveliness in her voice. Malu saw this as a softening of the blow from the news of his failure to win the job she was certain would be his.

"Radel has given him some medication to settle him for the night. He will return in the morning to see that he is taken to Pennson Hospital for further treatment."

"Is there anything else we can do?"

"Not really. Anyway, we will know tomorrow."

They both tried to avoid going where it would hurt to enter, so they spoke about the baby Cecala was expecting, how Mark and Abi would react to the new arrival and whether Cecala would like to have her delivery at home or at the Fanoh Nursing Home. As they engaged deeper into conversation about these matters, the coolness they had earlier displayed in each other's presence warmed into a relaxed gentleness that brought smiles at the mention by Malu, that Cecala's bun in the oven was not showing prominently after six months of incubation.

They had dinner together that night, with the children. Abi was propped up in a high chair at the head of the table. "I have three lectures to deliver tomorrow. I plan to deliver them as scheduled. It is business as usual for now, as far as I am concerned."

"Did you not say that you will be seeing Papa in the morning? How can you manage it with that lecture schedule?"

"Two of them will be in the afternoon. I will leave for the hospital after the morning lecture, which should last till 9.30 am."

"I'd like to see Papa too. I can go there earlier. Once I have dropped off the children at school, I'll set off to see Papa."

"Your presence will surprise him. I appreciate the effort."

"Thanks. But I cannot afford to lose such a supportive father-in-law."

They finished dinner and retired to their bedroom. Not a hint of the sadness of their morning's encounter remained.

Chapter 15

Madika was taken to Pennson Hospital by Dr. Radel
Lamara, early on Monday morning. He was in a dazed
state. There had been some deterioration in his
condition during the night. Using his influence as a
former senior doctor at Pennson, Madika was taken
directly to the intensive care unit of the hospital, bypassing the emergency department. Dr. Lamara
discussed Madika's case with the consultant cardiologist,
Dr. Martin Boya. Satisfied that he was in good hands, he
left the unit. He walked a few paces along the corridor,
then returned to give Boya his card and asked for his.
"Please keep me informed of his progress. The patient is
like a father to me," he said. Most of the morning was
taken up with tests to determine the cause of his poor
condition, deciding medication and setting up equipment
to monitor his vital functions.

Cecala arrived at the hospital just after 10.00 am. The
nurse attendant at the reception told her that her father-
in-law was in the Intensive Care Unit and that visits were
authorized only by the doctor in charge of the unit. It
took almost 45 minutes before she was allowed into the
unit and, only after she had made a call to her husband's
friend Dr. Radel Lamara. Lamara obtained permission
from Dr Boya for her to see her father-in-law, as a
special favour. A duty doctor escorted Cecala to the unit
after seeing that the attendant at the entrance had fitted
her with protective clothing and boots. He warned her
that she should not excite the patient in any way. She
moved in quietly and stood by Madika's bedside. He did

not recognize her at first. Then slowly the image became clearer. "Cecala, is that you," he cried. He tried to raise his hand to offer it to her, but it dropped back to his side.

"Don't move, Papa," she said. He wanted to say something, but Cecala pressed her finger to her lips. "No don't," she said. He smiled and nodded. She saw that his cheeks were sallow and he had a fixed stare. She spoke again in a low voice, as a nurse approached them. " You will be fine. The doctors and nurses are good here. They will get you over this hurdle." She judged from the assembly of tube and wires connected to his right hand and chest, that indeed the hurdle was a serious one. The nurse came over to her. "Excuse me miss. My name is Nurse Masa. I am assigned to this patient and the one opposite. I'd like to take some readings. If you don't mind, could you wait outside for a minute?" Cecala left the room and sat on one of the chairs outside by the door, presumably left there for the purpose. She was out of the room for only ten minutes, before the nurse called her back in.

"It was good that he was brought in when they did," Nurse Masa informed her. "Further delay would have made his condition irreversible," she added.

"Thank you."

"We will be monitoring his condition over the next few days and if we find it stable, we will transfer him to a normal ward to continue his treatment."

"My husband will be visiting him in the afternoon. I hope he too will be allowed to see him."

"I shall brief the duty doctor before I go off duty in case I am off duty when he arrives. We make concessions for immediate family. I am sure he will have no problem seeing him."

"Thank you, nurse, that's nice of you."

"I have given him some sedation. Once it takes effect, you can leave."

"I will be back tomorrow. We are very concerned about his condition. My husband feels guilty about his father's sudden ill health. He believes that he was responsible for causing it."

"Why is that?"

"I can't talk about it. It is a sensitive matter, which didn't go down well with Papa."

"I'm sorry. It happens in families. Some children blame themselves for not caring for their parents at times when it matters most to them."

"It is not that at all. In my husband's case, he loves his Papa. He cares for him even to the detriment of his own family. He is his father's favourite son and has often lived up to his father's expectation."

"Then he should be satisfied that he has done his best for him."

There was a loud scream coming from the bed opposite Madika's. The girl on the bed was pulling at the tubes connected to her body and kicking frantically at the bed covers. Nurse Masa dashed over to deal with the emergency. She pressed the alarm bell on the wall behind the girl's bed before approaching the troubled patient cautiously. She checked that the tubes were still in place and tried to calm her with words that seemed to halt the agitation; but for how long she thought. After a few minutes, she was shouting and kicking again. At that moment, four bulky ward assistants burst into the room and moved to the scene ready to apply any help needed. Seeing the drama unfolding before her, Cecala quickly walked out of the room and made her way to the exit.

Soon after his morning lectures, Malu returned home, hoping to find out from Cecala how her visit to the hospital earlier in the morning went. Cecala was not at home. Since she had her first child, Mark, she had given up her job at the Ministry of Foreign Affairs and become a full-time housewife. Malu wondered why she was not already home from the hospital. He did not expect her to be that late and she had not called. So, he thought that some crisis or other in her father's condition, may have caused her delay. Whatever the reason, it was worrying not to know. Determined to find out, he rushed out of the house into his car and was at the hospital within minutes of leaving his house. Cecala, however had thought that it was expedient for her to visit her parents and inform them of Madika's illness, while she was already in the city and not far from their home. She thought she could also stay with them and chat until it was time to collect her youngest child, Helen, from nursery. She failed to call home and report her changed plans, overlooking the negative impact that might have on Malu in his stage of anxiety.

At the reception, Malu was given clearance to see his father. He was escorted to the intensive care unit, adorned in the mandatory protective gear. When he was taken into the IC unit, the first thing that struck him was the silence, the brightness of the space that held twelve critically ill patients in bed on wheels, fixed in ordered regularity, as if to emphasize the seriousness of the business of the intensive care that went on within its walls. A nurse approached him from a desk at the far end of the room.

"Dr. Malu?" she said.

"I am. Good afternoon, nurse. I would like to see my father who was brought in this morning"

"I am Nurse Muna. I relieved Nurse Masa who was in the morning shift. I now have the responsibility to look after your father. Nurse Masa told me to expect your visit this afternoon."

"How did she know that?"

"She said that your wife was here this morning. Because she had difficulty getting permission to see your father, she asked me to help get you cleared at reception for your visit. That is how I know, doctor. Did you have any trouble coming through?"

"None. Thank you."

"Come with me doc."

They walked passed a line of beds, until they reached Madika's bed. It was screened off from view.

"We had an unexpected rise in his temperature an hour ago, but it is falling nicely now. We have had more tests done, following a review of his condition by Dr. Boya's team. He has been given additional medication, but we have to keep him calm and undisturbed."

"Can I see him for a while?"

"For a short while, yes; say ten minutes." She parted the screen a meter wide so Malu could see his father lying still and hooked up to machines in much the same way as Cecala had left him.

"As you can see, he is asleep now," the nurse said. "You could come back tomorrow. Hopefully, you would see him then. We are restricting the frequency of visits to avoid any relapse." She spoke these words with the cautiousness of a health professional.

He drove back home through the winding road leading to his residence on campus. It is still as dangerous as it was when the campus was first built. On the left of the road, the land rises steeply on to a plateau beyond, where elegant houses dominated the sparse woodlands, once cherished as a lover's hideout. Most of the trees have disappeared in the years of unregulated firewood harvesting. On the right, the land drops sharply into Whine Water River, a fast-flowing river that empties into Morue Bay. On its banks, tall trees and shrubs block the view of the sea from the narrow roadway. There are road signs every 400 metres, some displaying the speed limit of 20 kilometres per hour. Others warning motorists of sharp bends and steep gradients. These warnings have never deterred reckless drivers from speeding along this dangerous road and skidding off it into the gorge below. In the last year alone, three people have lost their lives in this way.

When he was near the bend into the bridge over Whine Water River, he saw a group of onlookers, standing by the edge of the roadway peering anxiously into the ravine below. On the other side of the road, a crowd had collected. Some in the crowd were stopping vehicles and appealing to drivers and their passengers to alight and render assistance. It appeared that something disastrous had occurred on the other side of the road where they stood. There were women in the crowd, screaming and wringing their hands in uncontrollable grief. He drew up behind a parked land rover vehicle and joined the crowd. Soon after he alighted from his car, the police arrived, waving other cars on, to keep the traffic moving.

A bulky man and two others, came from the crowd and appealed to drivers in the parked vehicles which carried tow ropes, to spare them for use in the rescue of a man trapped in his car in the ravine, on the other side of the road. They explained that they needed a long length of tough rope to deal with the emergency. There was panic as the men hurriedly joined the ropes they could secure, to get the length they required. They moved to the edge of the ravine with more men to help. Malu moved over with them, suggesting that he called the Fire Force which had the appropriate rescue equipment and experience to do the job. "We have called the station. They told us that they were on their way. That was twenty minutes ago, and this car is held precariously between two branches of a large tree overlooking the river. There is no telling when the branches will snap." One of the men spoke, he was obviously agitated.
"Can't you wait another five minutes? Your attempt might dislodge the car from the branches and make things worse," Malu said.
"See for yourself. The car is already tilting and will drop off at any moment. If we send him a rope now, he can wrap it around his waist, crawl out of the car and hold on to a more secure branch before the car drops off."

The men pushed Malu aside and proceeded to check the length of rope they had joined together, made a loop, and threw the life line down into the ravine. They swung it like a pendulum so that at each return swing, the rope would go past the open door of the car. On three instances when the rope swung past the driver's side of the car, the trapped man tried to grab it and failed. The impact of the car on projecting rocks as it cascaded down the side of ravine wrenched open the door of the car. Apparently, he was hesitant to step closer to the edge of the open door fearing that he might slip and fall into the depths below. Each time, he tried, he was too slow to reach the rope. It was only his right hand that was of any use and even that was sore. His left hand was dripping with blood. His body was bruised, and ached badly. He was in excruciating pain.

Luckily, his seat belt was still firmly locked in position. It kept him in the car. He would otherwise have been through out and have ended in the river lifeless. He knew that time was running out for him. The rescuers on the road were doing their best to help, but it was left to him to save himself. He released his seat belt cautiously and turned to face the door, placing his right hand in position for the next swing of the rope. As it came close to the door, he stretched out his right hand and caught it. He quickly slipped the loop over his head and tightened it around his waist. With only one hand usable, it took some twisting and turning to accomplish it. These movements rocked the car and made it more unstable. The rescuers shouted to him to jump from the car. It was tilting badly, but he remained seated looking out into the abyss. He seemed confused. They shouted louder, "Jump man! Jump!" He didn't hear them.

At this point, they had the rope taut, between them and his body. They placed a wooden platform they had quickly constructed ready to launch against the top of the gorge, so they could break the swing of the rope as it came off the car with the injured driver, then pull him up to safety. As they put the platform in place, the car slipped from the branches. Their creaking sound alarmed him. In fear of going down with the car, he swung his legs towards the door and let them hang limply over the edge of the open door. He was still afraid to jump. "Jump out man! Jump!" the cry came again. The men released more lengths of the rope to take in the drop. It became too long for the platform to be effective. Then suddenly it dawned on him that the shouting meant something. Before he could resolve this in his mind, it was too late. The car dropped away from him, and he was flung with frightening force against the exposed face of a rock on the other side of the ravine, the rope still tied around his waist. Shouts of anguish rose from the crowd of onlookers as they heard the cry of pain when his body hit the rock. Intermittent groans followed the crash; loud at first, then like an orchestrated diminuendo, they faded into silence.

The Fire Force arrived to find the men with the tow rope slowly pulling the lifeless body of the driver up the face of the ravine. The impact had dismembered the driver's body. Malu went to meet the fire officers as they unloaded their equipment.

"If you had been here earlier, this life would have been saved," he said.

"Sir, we came as soon as we could," the chief of the team replied.

"Well officer, we just lost a life. That makes it not soon enough."

"Today has been an unusual day for emergencies. We've had twelve calls so far and we have only a small force to deal with them."

"Sad, quite sad."

"If you don't mind sir, we must get on with our work." The chief moved away and directed his men to take over the retrieval of the dead body from the men who had been taking turns to pull the body up the deadly rock face.

Chapter 16

Malu reached home, depressed by what he had witnessed on his way home. Improving the city roads, had taken longer than the local government had promised. There were major construction projects going on in the central business district and in the north of the city, but roads leading to the hillside towns remained hazardous and poorly maintained. He vouched never again to use this road to and out of the city until it was rebuilt. His children were having lunch when he entered the dining room. He liked to be with his family at meal times. It had been a religion for him. He hopped into the room flapping his hands like a bird. He was pretending to fly like the bird in the story he told them the night before. Legend had it that a giant bird named Kunuka, ruled over a colony of spirit birds in a cave in the forest of Akanja overlooking the village of Relfont. This bird had antennas naturally set within its body, through which it received alarm waves from homes where there were disobedient children. At night, it would snoop into the target home, fly off with the children and keep them in the cave until they had learnt to behave. His mother had told him this story when he was a child. It was always a sobering warning that kept him from mischief. He kept a frightening image of this dreaded bird in his mind, so whenever his mother warned that Kunuka was noting his behaviour, he would quickly turn away from any act that could qualify as bad behaviour.

Malu sat down with the kids for a while, asking them about their day at school. Cecala had hoped to get the children fed and sent out into the garden before her husband returned home, so she could talk to him about her visit to his father at the hospital, without them eavesdropping into their conversation. Now she stood away from the table, angry that her plans had been frustrated. Realizing this, he ended his chat with the children and went over to meet Cecala.

He told her about the accident on Hills Road. "I just happened to be there minutes after the disaster happened. I will spare you the details, because it was too horrid to relate," he said. Then he took Cecala by the hand and led her slowly to their bedroom.

"You weren't home when I came back from the Institute. I had hoped to learn from you how Papa was doing before I left to see him. Anyway, I went to the hospital as planned. I could not stay long with him, but saw enough of his state, to make me very concerned about his condition."

"Well, when I saw him earlier, the nurse assigned to him, told me that there was no cause for alarm. I spoke to him briefly. He looked weak but dizzy. I think he had been asleep and had just woken up when I arrived."

"I will return to the hospital tomorrow to see him again."

"Darling, should we not inform the wider family of Papa's illness? We would be blamed, if they were told nothing and things got worse."

"I guess so, but as you know, I am not an extended family person. I am not in touch with any family other than my Aunts Banie and Macile. As for the family in Numbaya, where my parents come from, I have been kept isolated from them. When I was little, my parents had the odd family member visiting from the village, but that ended long before I finished primary school."

"At least, these aunts in Munga know of Papa's illness. However, they are entitled to have an update on their brother's illness."

"Those two are weird. Aunty Macile is weirder. We need to keep them out of the picture for the time being, till Papa is showing signs of improvement, otherwise, they will descend on the hospital and God knows what havoc they will cause there."

Cecala found it strange that her husband's family was so disunited. Village people always have united families. She could see from his countenance that he was feeling uncomfortable talking about family. Her family was united. In fact, so closely knit, that nothing happened with anyone in the family without the entire Josola clan knowing about it and working together to deal with any fallouts. When she was married, the supporters from Malu's family could occupy only a row of pews in the church. In contrast, her family filled every pew on the rows allocated to the bride's family and almost half of the pews allocated to the bridegroom's family. It was their friends who occupied the remaining pews. Cecala wanted to ask whether there were children from Auntie Macile's turbulent marriage, who could be contacted, but thought that would be treading on dangerous ground. He asked instead, "Have you ever thought of tracing your brother in the mines, since you came back from your studies overseas?"

The question took Malu by surprise. It bothered his conscience. He had not made any effort to get information about his brother's whereabouts before he left for his studies. He had thought of making a search for information that may put all the uncertainties in the family's mind to rest, but the pressure of academic life had prevented him from doing much about it. Like the rest of the family, he had accepted that his brother was dead. The family had painfully accepted the information received from his workmate and friend, that he was a victim of a mines attack by rival mining gangs. Discussion of the fates of Ganeh Coney and Simfa Coney were never entertained in their house. Malu could not reply. Cecala spoke again.

"His father is critically ill. It is a shame no one has ever tried to confirm the tragic news."

"Father must have tried. Knowing him, he would have explored every avenue possible to find out," Malu replied.

He wondered whether it was worth talking about tracing him now, with so much demand on our time to see Pa through this crisis in his life.

Cecala noticed his discomfort entertaining questions about his brother and turned to another subject, still about his family. She should have realized that this would be just as upsetting to her husband, but pressed on.

And your sister?" Cecala asked.

"That's another story. There has been a family feud over her disappearance since I was in primary school."

"That's sad. Why has it still not been resolved?"

"Because my Pa threatened to take my maternal grandmother to court, for abduction and murder of his daughter."

"You have not spoken about this before. How could the family live with this uncertainty all these years?

"I have not spoken about it because it is a matter that is kept tightly locked within the vault in which my parents keep the family's misfortunes. The fighting goes on fiercely but no one outside the four walls of our parent's bedroom knows how bad the row is."

"It must rob them of the joy of living, missing a child under circumstances that are unclear. And you were satisfied to have things as they are mute, blank, closed lipped?"

"All I knew was that I had a sister who was sent to her grandmother for womanhood initiation and decided to remain with her grandparents in the village. That is the story my mother likes to leak out, although inside she is hurting from her decision to yield to pressure from the child's grandmother."

Cecala was troubled by these revelations. She had found Malu's mother warm and cheerful whenever they were together. She got on very well with her. She loved her grandchildren. She and Malu often invited her to spend time with them and the children in their home, so she could get away from the noise of Munga. She would teach the children songs she had learnt as a child in the village and tell them gripping tales from ancient times.

Her father-in-law, on the other hand, was never relaxed in their home. He always felt out of place when he visited, so he never paid more than a day's visit. "I can't raid my daughter-in-law's kitchen, as I do my wife's," he revealed to Malu once, when he insisted that he stayed for the night, after a long day's visit. Rose was more outgoing. When she visited, she took over most of the household chores from Cecala, and supervised the house help. Her daughter-in-law sometimes wondered, why her mother-in-law kept herself so busy with housework and gave so much attention to their children, when she visited them. Now she believed that it was a mechanism she devised to keep her mind away from opening her hidden vault of misfortunes.

Cecala wanted to have more answers from her husband about his lost sister. She asked cautiously, "If your sister had stayed in the village on her own volition, why did she not make occasional visits home or send messages? She would know she had a younger brother whom she had not seen for ages. She would like to know how they and her parents were faring. That puzzles me."

"I know. The rumour is that she died during the initiation rite. Her grandmother was scared to tell my parents, so said nothing about it for a long time. Then she just disappeared. No one knew to what part of the country she had absconded."

"Was your brother kept in the dark about the truth surrounding his sister, as you were?"

"He must have resigned himself to accepting the lie we were all fed. No one talks about it anymore. It occurred so long ago, it is not worth digging up the pieces, my parents had buried deep in their vault."

Chapter 17

The past three days had left Malu emotionally drained, but he showed an outward strength of will power to fight against the flood of events that threatened to erode the foundations of his marriage. His wife seemed to have made her father-in-law's health her immediate concern. This pleased Malu. His father's sudden illness had mellowed the sourness Cecala felt after his defeat in the race to win the institute's highest office. She inwardly believed that the recent calamities in their lives, were precipitated by errors of judgement, for which she blamed Malu. While accepting that the new family crisis had put other issues on the backburner, she knew they would come back to occupy a prominent place in the order of disagreements between them.

Malu had been to see his father every day during the three weeks of his admission at Pennson hospital. Before he left for the hospital on the start of the fourth week, he telephoned his friend, Dr. Lamara to find out if there was any information from the hospital that he could share with him before he left home. Lamara told him that he had spoken to Dr. Boya

"I spoke to Dr. Boya, the cardiology consultant in charge an hour before Malu called. Boya had given him encouraging report on his father's condition. If he continued to improve throughout the day, the consultant told him, he would have Madika transferred to the general cardiology ward sometime the following day.

When Malu arrived at his father's bedside, he found him lying still. The last time he visited, the top end of his hospital bed was inclined at about 30%. He was breathing rapidly and loudly. There were tubes popping out of his chest and arms. Now, the bed was set in its normal horizontal position. Only the tube on his right arm was still in place.

"Papa," he said. "I am so glad to see you looking so much better than when you were brought in."

"The doctors think that I have made some improvement. I definitely feel stronger now."

"All you have to do now is leave things to the doctors. They are the experts."

"How is Ma doing? Tell her I'll be home soon. We have had our problems, but she is a good lady.' His eyelids half dropped as he turned to look at Malu. He wanted to hold his hand, but found that raising his left hand which was next to the seat Malu occupied, hurt.

"Come over here, son." Madika moved his head in the direction of the chair on the other side of the bed. Malu moved over. He pulled the chair and sat on it. Then as if on cue, his father pulled out his right hand from under the crisp white sheets that covered his body and touched Malu on the forehead, then his left shoulder. He looked up but could not make his eyes meet his father's, so he looked away and placed his hand on his father's, which was still clutching the round of his shoulder. No one spoke for a while. Then overcome by the emotion, he began to cry. A few tears rolled down his cheeks at first, then a shudder of his upper body released the pain he had bottled within his troubled self, since his last visit to

166

his parents in Munga. His shirt sleeves took the full volume of that later flood. When it stopped to flow, he removed his hand from his father's and reached for a handkerchief in his trousers pocket. In the quietness of the space that engulfed them both, Malu's sobs hit Madika like a clap of thunder, punching his father's senses and releasing old memories. He thought of the day he cried loudly in his bedroom. That was the time he blamed himself for the loss of their daughter. He regretted that he had lacked the firmness then to resist the pressure put on him by his wife, to allow their daughter to leave home and be lost to them.

He looked at his son, as he wiped off the traces of tears from his cheeks. As their eyes met, he said, "Son don't lay any blame on yourself. The greater blame is on me." He removed his hand from his son's shoulder and tucked it back under the folds of the bed cloth. His hand secured under the linen, "I love you, son, he said. Without you, I have no life of honour. I was nothing even to those who had nothing. You made me something among those who count for many things." Malu sat for another ten minutes, not saying a word.

The nurse in charge broke the silence. "Excuse me, it is time for me to administer the patient's medication and record his vital signs." Malu moved to the foot of the bed and watched the nurse perform her tasks. On completing the procedure, she left, warning Malu not to keep his Papa engaged in conversation, because he was still weak and under a carefully controlled medical regime. His father heard the warning and smiled.

"The nurses have their ways," he said.

"It is the hospital's policy she is following, Papa. Visits of non-medical people to the intensive care unit are limited. I understand that. Papa, you were very ill."

He had escaped death by a very small margin. The nurses had to ensure that no one caused their patient any upset that would result in a relapse into an unmanageable situation. Visitors sometimes fail to appreciate the risks to patients, by their presence.

As he rose to leave, his father said, "Please thank Radel for his effort in getting me here and monitoring my care. He has been here every morning to see me and to consult with the doctors on my case."

"I will," he said. "Radel is a trustworthy friend and a doctor of immense experience. He will never see you ill, Papa and treat you like a stranger. I know he will do everything to get you back to full health."

"Thank you, son. Don't forget to take care of your mother, you hear me? You and your mother; that's all I've got now, you know."

"I know Papa, but please don't think about us just yet. You need to get well. That's paramount."

His father's illness had a devastating effect on him. He could not get over the feeling that he was responsible for his present condition. He knew that his father loved him so much that he had given him all the encouragement he needed to achieve all he had. It hurt him to see his father fighting to recover from the illness he felt he had caused. It had crushed something within him that used to glow in his presence. Now darkness threatened to ruin the future to which he had aspired. He had all kinds of thoughts crowding his mind. He had to keep silent until his father spoke. He told him that God would make new light to shine within him and inspire him to become the beacon of knowledge that he was meant to be. After another spell of silence, Malu started walking away.

He couldn't bring himself to leave his father, so he returned and sat down by his bedside, his head bowed. Something was erupting again within him that he was suppressing. Suddenly it burst out into tears, his body trembling as drops of tears rolled down his cheeks and landed on the grey tiles on the unit's floor. "You must go son; your wife and children need you." He faintly heard his father's voice. It sounded like an instruction, but Malu interpreted it as a charge for him to do the right thing for the happiness of his family. He drove home from the hospital dejected. Avoiding the Hill Road, he took the Ridge Road into the village of Marrup, and out again, bypassing the village playground and on to the road leading to the Kilinde campus.

Chapter 18

Malu had rescheduled his classes for the day, so he could see his father as usual and then visit his mother at Munga. What time of the day he had left, he would spend working on his new research on the Mali Empire, a Mandinka/Bambara empire in West Africa. He was researching the period from 1230 to1600. The empire was founded by Sundiata Keita and became renowned for the wealth of its rulers, especially under Mansa Musa. The Mali Empire profoundly influenced the culture of West Africa through the spread of its language. Malu had studied the early period from 1230 -1430, its conquests and its wealth and had started to expand his research on the rulers of the period, particularly Mansa Musa its founder. The influence of the empire was felt over many parts of West Africa, reaching his own country where the language of the empire still survives in the north-western part of the country. He thought that it was important for him to complete this work, before he took any decision about his future. He was the leading authority on African history in the country. His departure from Kilinde would adversely affect the stature of the department in the country and overseas. He had not ventured into this dark room of potential contention with Cecala, since they were hit with the news of his failed shot at the top job at Kilinde. He wanted to be clear about his plans to leave, before taking on that challenge.

Cecala greeted him as he came through the door into the sitting room. In her mind, she harboured so many confusing thoughts. The most worrying was the health of her father-in-law. With her husband having the day off from lectures, she reckoned that there was time to deal with that issue before she left home to pick up the kids from school. Unsmiling, she gave him a little hug and kissed him on both cheeks. As she did so, she saw the tear stains above where she had kissed him and the redness of his eyes, revealing the hurt he concealed in the enforced smile he served out when she hugged him.

"You have been crying, Mal," she said. She spoke with a raised voice, recalling his distraught countenance the day before, when he reported seeing a gruesome accident on Hill Road. She wanted to hear news from the hospital, not a display of emotion from him on another of his encounters with tragic accidents. She looked at him again and realized that his state of sadness must have come from a personal grief, not from any reaction from a distant tragedy.

"Are you all right? Is Papa ok?" she asked.

"There is no cause for alarm, as far as I can judge," he replied

"But you; what's wrong?"

"I'm just worried about how much I have to do to finish the paper on the research I have been struggling with for months now. I don't see me meeting the deadline for presenting this paper, with my mind the way it is right now." He nervously waited for what was coming.

"All you think of is work. Your father is ill. I am carrying our third child and getting sick like a dog holding on to it, and you worry about a paper you propose to deliver to some spurious conference. You disgust me!"

"Sorry darling, don't take it so badly, I think we should calmly talk these things over like mature people."

"You can think what you like, but I am leaving to pick up the children from school." She walked past him into their bedroom and returned with the keys to her car. She drove straight to her parent's house, where she often waited till the school's closing time.

The moment her mother opened the front door, she fell into her arms crying. "What's troubling you, Sweetie?" Her mother always called her Sweetie, because of her happy disposition. She was her mother's closest friend and confidante. They were very close. She remembered her growing up with her two brothers and being so loved because she was so dependable. She was only twelve, when she was beginning to show signs of responsibility. Without fuss or complaint, she would voluntarily take on housework her brothers hated, helping her with everything she wanted done around the house. During the first twelve months following her father's mine accident, her mother found it difficult to cope with the emotional stress and the intensive care he needed after his discharge from hospital. It was Cecala, as young as she was then, who strengthened her will to deal with the challenges of that bleak period in her life. She approached everyone with a smile. As she matured into an adult, her beautiful dark tan skin, her natural charm, and her ease in speaking to adults and her peers alike, endeared her to many members of the expanded Josola family. She was the one who always volunteered to take charge, when there were family functions to organize. In the embrace in which mother and daughter were fused, many past experiences were exchanged; none of them in words.

Releasing herself from the embrace, she said, "Mama, Malu has been a bloody beast. He is unconcerned about my condition and indifferent about the state of his father's illness."

"I am surprised, Sweetie. I find him charming and generous. As far as I can see, he has been a good provider, giving you and your children all the comforts of life."

"True, but one has to look ahead. The way he is going, he could puncture the love we have nourished all these years, with utter confidence in each other. Until now, we have kept no secret from each other. He is changing, Mama. I once believed that our love for each other was perfect; an example to our young friends and kids. Now I worry about that and about our future"

"What can be so wrong? Are you not being too pessimistic? All of us have minor imperfection in physical looks and in our characters."

"No, no, no, Mama. Recently, he has been behaving as though he has no regard for my feelings, or regard for my intelligence. He came home half-an-hour ago, looking miserable. He had the audacity to lie that it was his work that was worrying him."

"If indeed he was hiding something from you, could it not be that he wants to protect you from information that would upset you?"

"What is marriage about then, if husband and wife cannot share their griefs as well as their joys?"

"You mean, keeping to the marriage pledge, 'for better for worse; for richer or poorer'?"

"Yes, that is a commitment married people must keep ensuring that trust is fully established in the married home."

"Sweetie, I must tell you that there are limits to the extent to which some of us honour our marriage pledge."

"But that is not right. For most women, marriage is a serious commitment and they are very sensitive to violations of this pledge."

Her mother looked at her, stretched out her hands to touch her shoulders. She led her to a seat in the hallway and sat next to her. "Look here," she said, then continued, slowly collecting her thoughts, "I found out something interesting about life. That is, not to judge anyone by their first mistake. When your Papa and I were just married, we spent most Friday evenings at a night spot called The Manga Club. It was run by two of his friends. The place was always packed full of couples and single people having a good time.

During one of these Friday night outs at the club, one of them approached me for a dance. With your Papa's permission, he escorted me to the floor and we danced to the music then playing. The music ended and I was returning to my seat when he held me back to dance to the next piece. In the dim light of the club, he danced closer to me in the rhythm of the deafening sound of a song I liked. Even though it was dim, your Pa saw this man pressing his face against mine. He concluded that we were in a love grip and kissing each other. As soon as I returned to my seat, he told me that we were leaving. I picked up my bag and we were out of that place in no time, never to return. He was furious. Back home, he blamed me for being too permissive of the man's obvious advances. He said that I was foolish and unfaithful. I told him that nothing he saw was consensual. The man had forced himself on me. I only tried to behave politely as he was Gorbe's friend. I insisted that I felt nothing for him.

The week that followed was a nightmare. In frustration over those continuing arguments, I threatened to leave him. Eventually, he saw reason, and admitted his mistake. Look at his condition now. I was only thirty-two, when his accident happened. Few women that age would sacrifice their entire active years looking after someone so badly handicapped. That is what love does, imperfect as it often is. It makes you sacrifice many things for its sake." Cecala turned to her mother and said, "Mama, you surely are one patient, strong and lovable person. Your story amazes me."

"You are strong too" her mother said. Patience is an anathema to the young. But like the dew, it shows as droplets in the evening of our years. Come, let me sit you out with your Papa while I get you both something to eat."

They walked through the sitting room into the back yard. She greeted her father and took a seat by him. He was reclining on a cane chair, reading the day's Clendon

Chronicle newspaper. "I will be back," her mother said, walking into the house.

"What good news have you brought us?" Her father asked her, keeping his eyes on the newspaper.

"Nothing exciting," she said. "I am just stopping by as usual to later pick up the kids from school. You are the one getting all the news." She kept her problems away from her dad.

"Not all, but you must have heard the news that Mandela has been elected president of South Africa, following the first multiracial elections, in which the ANC won a majority. It was on the radio yesterday, but it is in the newspaper today," her father said.

"I listened to the report of the election in the news last night. It is refreshing to receive good news from our African neighbours after the April 6th report of the Rwanda massacre."

"Such diabolical happenings are setting the continent back. We have continuing problems of sectionalism, intolerance, selfishness, and greed. If we fail to wipe these out of our various countries, the independence we gained from the colonial powers will mean nothing, and we will lose respect in the world."

Shorbu returned with two plates of fried plantains and beans. "Have a break. Stop the politics, "she said. "It's time to eat." She served out the food. She sat with them as they ate, all three looking out into the yard. Beyond the boundary wall, the rays of the afternoon sun were struggling to come through the branches of the large apple tree at the edge of the small garden patch on which Shorbu grew green vegetables and tomatoes. She usually has the help of a part-time house boy from the neighbourhood. At about 2.30 p. m., Cecala asked to be excused. She had been given a dose of confidence to get on with her life. She drove from her parent's house to collect her children from school. They were already out of the building and playing with their friends in the school's grounds when she arrived. The children safely in the car, she drove home, wondering how to confront Malu on his elusiveness towards her. She believed that she had gained some wisdom from her conversation with her mother. That should place her in good stead.

Malu was in his study when he heard the noise of the kids as they streamed into the house. At 3.30 p.m., Cecala called him to the table for lunch. They ate with the children. Cecala waited nervously for her husband to say something. Instead, it was the children who kept themselves entertained during the meal. He was not his usual self. He looked bored throughout the chitchatting and teasing that went on around him. When he finished eating he got up and left the table, saying to Cecala, "We must talk." She heard the terseness in his voice and wondered whether that was the same man he had loved dearly all those past years. It sounded to her like a notice to get herself prepared for war. She knew that none of them could engage in any kind of lovers' battle and survive.

The hours after lunch dragged on. She had her normal routine with the children: home work for the older kids, playtime in the garden, then off to bed. Often, Malu would join them in the garden and then they would all

177

have dinner together. That day was different. He was locked in his study till 7.00 p.m., when he walked into the back patio where Cecala was sitting reading the Jeffrey Archer novel, 'As the Crow Flies'. She and her husband were avid readers of novels. They chose a day each month when they discussed the books they had read that month.

"May I take your mind off your book for a moment?" He said it casually, as he came to her from the back of her chair.

"Sure," she said. He walked past her and sat on another chair.

"Firstly," he said, "you owe me an apology for your insulting remarks to me this morning."

"I could equally say that you too owe me an apology. You lied to me."

"No. All I did was trying to avoid sharing the unbearable load of misery I brought with me from the hospital. You interpreted me wrongly." Cecala's eyes were searching every visible part of her husband's body, to find out if his words told anything that was going on in his mind; vengeance, compromise, placation, whatever.

In a way, they shared the same passion for honesty and openness. Those had been the principles which had directed their lives. She knew that too many recent events had tested their commitment to those principles, and affected the rhythm of their lives. She felt that they should find ways to regain what they had lost. She was silent for a long time, during which she thought of episodes in the book she was reading, where dishonesty and rivalry affected relationships across many situations;

war, business, and love included. She raised her head and moved her search to his face. He could not associate the face in her view with the dishonesty she had earlier charged him with. There was a glint in his eyes which made her believe that he had it in him to forget the happenings of the morning. Before she could speak a word, she saw him rise from his seat and dash into the kitchen. He came back with two wine glasses half full of clear natural water. "Let's make peace," he said. They drank to that. Then they sat talking in the faded light of the night till long after midnight, their body language telling each other that all was well. They must take on their morning commitments, groggy from going to bed late; she with the kids and he at Pennson to observe the transfer of his father to a general ward.

Part 4
Imperfect Direction

Chapter 19

The Okeju Evangelical Church had been holding evening prayer meetings on Wednesdays, since the church was established in Munga in 1982. When Madika and Rose became members of the church, they regularly attended these evening meetings of prayer and healing. During the last six weeks since Madika's illness, Rose had been unable to attend without her husband, although Pastor Elijah had tried many times to persuade her to attend. He had offered to have her escorted back home by a church elder, each time she attended, so she could feel safe walking back to her home in the dark. She had always turned him down, saying, "It is not the dark that keeps me away, Pastor, it is missing Madika by my side with his hand pressed against mine as we pray that prevents me from attending. That closeness always raises me up to fully experience the overwhelming power of the holy spirit upon me."

Only a week earlier, when Pastor Elijah visited her at her home to enquire about progress with Madika's recovery, he had told her that with faith, everything was possible, that Madika would rise from his sick bed and be strong again.

"No enemy, no demon will stop that from happening," he said. "You have the strength within you to experience that power and use it with the combined faith of your prayer group to ask for Madika's full recovery,"

"I fear most times, that I will lose him to the angels. He has been so ill," she replied.

181

"Rose, we have never stopped believing that he will recover. We pray for his full recovery at every one of our regular church services."

"Thank you, Pastor. I know that you have always been our rock and salvation in times of grief. Next Wednesday, God willing, you will see me back at evening prayer.

That Wednesday, Rose had planned to attend the Okeju Evangelical Church prayer meeting, but that afternoon, Malu had sent word to her, that he would be visiting her in the evening, after seeing his father at the hospital. Rose could not therefore attend the prayer meeting. She was anxious to receive up-to-date news about her sick husband.

The prayer meeting was fully attended. Evening prayer meetings were held in the small chapel, built as an annex to the main chapel. There were four other buildings on the mission grounds, all sited opposite the chapels. One of them was the Pastor's Retreat, a two-storey elegant structure with two imposing marble pillars framing the entrance to the ground floor. On the east end of the building, a wide spiral staircase of stainless steel and polished mahogany timber leads directly to the second floor. This building stood apart from the three other buildings which made up this mission complex. One of these was a four-storey block of residential apartments for resident elders. Next to it was a large multipurpose hall named after the prophet Moses. The third was the mission's business centre. This was also a four-storey building with seminar and lecture rooms on the three top floors and the Church Administration on the ground floor. This floor also housed the Pastor's office and private study.

With so many members giving testimonies and so many miracle healings performed during the meeting, the pastor was exhausted and went straight to bed after eating a light super. At about twelve mid-night, security guards in mission compound were startled by an unusually loud noise and shouting, outside the mission gate. When they went out to investigate the disturbance, they found traders clamouring to get into a truck from which a man was alighting. He was dirty and frail. He clutched a crumpled leather bag under his left arm. He said that he had been travelling all night to reach the mission. The driver had been kind to bring him there, as it was too late for him to walk to the mission from the lorry park alone. He said that he was desperate and needed to see Pastor Elijah. He had travelled all night on a succession of goods trucks from one town to another, as free rides become available. Seeing his poor condition, drivers had taken pity on him, allowing him to squeeze into whatever free space was available between their load of goods. He looked nothing like the church members, who paid visits to the pastor.

Driven by sympathy for the man and his desperate condition, they went back to the security post to consider whether his was a case that was serious enough to wake up anyone in the mission to attend to it. But their loyalty and discretion escaped testing that night, when they saw the pastor walking towards them. The shouting at the gate had prematurely got him out of bed. He enquired from the guards what the trouble was. They told him that there was a man, in a miserable state, at the gate pleading to be allowed to see him. The Pastor was surprised that anyone so wretched could have known his name, and where to find him. However, out of curiosity and compassion, he asked the security workers to let him in. As soon as he was within a metre or so of the pastor, he knelt and burst into tears. The pastor took his hand, raised him up and said. "Stand up brother, who are you?"

"My name is Ganeh Koney, son of Madula and Rose Koney," he said

"But why are you here at this hour of the night."

"Hearing that my father was sick and dying, I wanted to see him before he dies."

"But why here?"

"I know that my parents are members of Okeju Evangelical Church. I was hopeful that if I found my way to the church's mission, and saw you, you would be able to help me see him and my family, whom I have deserted for over twenty years."

He gave the pastor a brief account of his life away from home. He told how he sneaked out of home unknown to his parents and went off to work in the mines in a neghbouring country; how he was cheated out of his earnings by devious workmates and how he had to escape from the mining area to a safe border town, to avoid being killed by former mining colleagues who believed that he had hidden money from the sale of minerals they had mined together. He had gone through a series of heart breaking experiences which left him bankrupt. He confessed that he connived with friends to send false information to his parents, giving them the impression that he had been killed, when in truth, he had escaped and was living with friends. They had protected him until he could travel to Munga.

He could not stop crying as he spoke. "I realize, that it will be difficult to get forgiveness from my parents for the pain I have caused them," he said. "But I have an aunt. Her name is Macile. She is one of the god parents I had at my baptism, who showed me much kindness in my childhood days. Pastor, if only she was told of my desperate condition, she would be glad to help calm the storm I have caused by my behaviour." When he had finished speaking Pastor Elijah said, "Brother you are in God's compound, we shall do all we can to get you accepted back into your family." He called one of his attendants, Joshua, and asked him to provide Ganeh with water, soap and towel for bath and give him food and a bed. Then he said to Ganeh, "We will get you some new clothes and see to your other needs in the morning," Ganeh replied in a faint voice, "Thank you sir. Praise God!"

****

At morning light, Pastor Elijah, asked one of his assistants to have Ganeh brought to his private study where he saw parishioners with personal prayer requests. He questioned him further about his life before leaving for the mines. He wanted to know why he deliberately caused his parents such grief. Ganeh was a grown man of 50 years. The previous night, he looked grey and shrivelled like a vagrant. He was clean shaven now and in clean clothes provided by Joshua, but they hung loose over him like a shroud. His eyes were unsteady. He seemed unable to look the Pastor straight in the eye as he answered questions about himself. As he spoke, Pastor Elijah made notes on the mission's book of testimonies.

Satisfied that he had recorded all that Ganeh was prepared to tell, Pastor Elijah rose from his chair, stretched out his hands and took Ganeh's. He then led him to the prayer circle in the middle of his study and asked him to kneel. He said a prayer for his redemption from all the sins he had committed and asked that God would direct him along the path of righteousness for the rest of his days. At the end of the prayer he said to Ganeh, "I would like you to attend our morning service today. There were three daily services at the church, I will ask Joshua to take you to the first service, which starts at 8.30 a.m. You should be ready as soon as you have taken breakfast with our resident elders. This is often ready at 7.30 a.m. in the compound's Moses Hall."

Immediately after his meeting with Ganeh, Pastor Elijah held his regular Church Committee meeting with his elders. During the meeting, he briefed them about the unexpected arrival at the mission the night before. He told them of his meeting with Ganeh earlier, and his request that he should help him reach reconciliation with his family. The pastor informed the meeting that he intended to visit Ganeh's family after he had conducted the early morning service. "I would like Evangelist Samuels to stand in for me at the second and third services of the day." he told the meeting. Samuels was an inspiring preacher and counsellor. He had been in the church for fifteen years and was now one of Pastor Elijah's trusted colleagues. The morning services were not always well attended. But word had gone around that Madika and Rose's son had unceremoniously surfaced from nowhere. Many wanted to see for themselves if that was true and how this prodigal son looked. Before the service started, members were milling around the pews chatting mostly about Madika and Rose and how they would react to the news of their son's arrival at the mission. There were comment and condemnation heard from several small groups gathered around some of the windows on the north and south walls of the temple. Everyone in the temple could hear them. Those feeling aggrieved by Ganeh's disrespect for his parents, were more vociferous. Some were making scurrilous remarks about his behaviour. Many were friends of his parents. One of them, a woman who lived on the same street as Madika and Rose said, "How can a grown up man like him just turn up like that and expect to be forgiven instantly? He has no conscience." "Poor Rose!" They wished she could hear their concern for her. They were worried that a lost son, dropping in as he had done without any notice, would give his mother the shock of her life and that might kill her. As for Ganeh, he was desperate to to reconcile with his parents. That was a sign that he had regretted his actions and wanted

187

the church to reach out to him and help him through his rehabilitation.

As if orchestrated by a conductor, everyone stopped speaking when Joshua walked into the temple with Ganeh by his side. They stared at his wrinkled face. It was possible to identify him, even though the years of hardship, intrigues, and violence in the brutal arena of artisan mining had left him frail and older than his years. The interior of the chapel was more majestic than the entrance. Ganeh was awe struck by the beauty of the surrounding into which he was led. Joshua chose a seat at the rear of the temple. The Pastor started the service with his usual flowery welcome, calling on the Almighty to receive the prayers and supplications of his children. He was moving his hands upwards, outwards and forwards, as he spoke. His loud voice echoed from the dome, shaped perfectly to reflect all the sounds that this assembly could generate.

It was the Pastor's voice that dominated the air waves for the first ten minutes of the service. He was a tall man with an athletic build. He used it to great effect, moving sprightly from one end of the altar to another. He told the congregation that they had in their midst one whom God had directed to them for relief from the enormous burden he had carried for most of his life. "This is God's way, not ours. Let us rejoice in his power and his will as we witness the redemption he has decreed for this repentant soul," he said and raised a chorus. Ganeh felt uncomfortable in his seat. The congregation was standing, all of them joining in the chorus, clapping and dancing to the rhythm of the song. "Get up and dance," Joshua told Ganeh, elbowing him. He rose and dreamily began to sway, with the congregation, but was tight-lipped. He had not been in a church of any description for ages. He knew not a word of the song.

When Pastor Elijah thought that he had stirred up enough frenzy in the crowd of worshippers, he started moving from one end of the large circular altar at the west end of the chapel to the other, shaking every part of his body. Then he started moving towards the east of the temple, dancing slowly and twisting his body like a boneless animal. As he passed each row of pews, his followers joined him. They were waving their hands as if to greet a descending angel. Some women in the dancing column were waving their shawls over his head shouting "Hallelujah, Hallelujah, Praise the Lord". By the time, he reached the pew in which Ganeh and Joshua were sitting, almost the whole congregation were out of their seats, singing and dancing with him. They enclosed him within a moving mass of unwavering believers. Their faces expressed the intense and passionate feeling of their commitment to their faith.

No one told them what to do when Pastor Elijah broke from the crowd and embraced Ganeh. They surrounded the two of them and burst into shouts of," Praise God, the redeemer reigns!" Then as the pastor took Ganeh's hand and began the long march to the altar, the accompanying congregation clapped and cheered. They reached the altar singing enthusiastically all the way. Then the pastor turned around and requested calm. The congregation moved to their seats leaving Ganeh standing alone in front of the altar facing the pastor.

The sound of music from the church's electronic organ slowly rose from the north-east corner of the church where it had been installed a year earlier, replacing the grand piano bought when the church was built. The decision to install an electronic organ was reached after a long debate on whether to follow the tradition of many established churches to install a pipe organ. Supporters of an electronic organ had argued that it had the capacity to reproduce a variety of sounds including that of a pipe organ, percussion, and orchestral instruments. Their argument had won the day and had made music at Okeju Evangelical as grand as it was.

Against the background of soft music, the pastor delivered his message. His theme was 'forgiveness in the face of imperfections in the future to which mankind often aspires.' He made many references to Ganeh and his failed ambition. "It is God who creates the perfect future. It is not within the power of man to determine the quality of that future," Pastor Elijah said. Ganeh stood silently throughout the fifteen minutes of the pastor's sermon. Whenever mention was made of any of his ordeals, he would bow his head nesting it between his hands. At the end of the sermon, the pastor invited four elders to join him as he laid his hands on Ganeh,

He prayed aloud for a transformation in his life. As he prayed there were echoes of supportive chants coming from the congregation, accompanied by drumming. The combination of sounds threw Ganeh into a panic. He was shaking like one during an epileptic feat. The elders held him to keep him from falling. The drumming grew progressively louder, forcing the pastor to raise his voice above the pitch of the drum beats. He spoke fast for spiritual effect, articulating many words in quick succession. Ganeh could hear only a few of them clearly.

"I free you from the clutches of Satan," he shouted

"Amen, Praise the Lord," the congregation shouted back in response.

"You are in the midst of prayer in the temple of righteousness."

"Hallelujah! Hallelujah!"

"Talk to God. Confess any wrongdoing you have committed and let peace dwell within you."

The congregation applauded, waving their hands in the air.

Ganeh, still being supported by the four elders, looked up to Pastor Elijah and whispered, "There is something important I must say to give me the peace I badly need."

"Believe that God loves you. The Holy Spirit will guide you to reveal all that have been kept locked in your mind all these years. No doubt they may have contributed to the strains that have wrecked your health," Pastor Elijah said.

The drumming and the organ music stopped as the pastor announced that Ganeh was going to give a testimony. The congregation applauded again. Some shouted, "Go on brother! God is with you."

Pastor Elijah handed him a microphone. The organ played a few chords as an introduction to his testimony. They seem to energise him. But this did not last. He became so nervous, overwhelmed by all that was happening around him, that he spoke for only three minutes.

He started by saying,
"Let me tell thanks to Almighty God for his goodness in bringing me to this holy temple from the deep hole of despair and suffering in which I was trapped. I thank Pastor Elijah for accepting me into the mission to free me from myself. I thank you all for your wonderful support of such a wretch like me."
"We love you son." Someone in the congregation shouted in a loud voice.
"With my own eyes, I witnessed evil of every description done to others and to me, in our desire to make something out of our lives. With vicious hate, my enemies destroyed my life and I, ruined by their influence, committed crimes I now regret," he continued.
"Praise the Lord," the congregation roared.
"You have heard the story of their treachery from Pastor Elijah. I will not repeat it. But I know now that God made my escape from death and my return home, possible."
"Give God the Glory." The congregation again, shouted in unison.

There was anticipation of what more Ganeh had to say. He could feel it in the air. He closed his eyes, not wanting to see the reaction of the congregation as he spoke. After a brief hesitation, he spoke.

"Yes, I will," he tried to shout back, but he was trembling; his voice was weakening. He could no longer stand erect. He opened his eyes for a moment and moved closer to the altar. He held on to the shiny brass railing that borders it, then closed his eyes again. He continued to speak, making a strenuous effort to be clearly heard.

"And I beg for his forgiveness," he said. "For in my distress, some of those with whom I started together laughed at me. I had forsaken my mother and father. I had let my family down. In shame and confusion, I wanted to die. After two unsuccessful attempts to end my life, I decided to fake it. As I have confessed to Pastor Elijah earlier, I sent a false message home to my parents as if coming from a friend, saying that I had been killed in the mines and buried without any ceremony by strangers. I did not care anymore if I never saw them again. May God forgive me for this heartless deceit."

There were groans of "God have mercy! God have mercy," coming from the pews.

At the end of his testimony, he asked the congregation for their understanding and sympathy. "I am not worthy of the welcome you have given me, but God has been merciful to me and for that I shall sing his praises till the end of my days."

The continuous loud applause which followed his testimony, was heard everywhere in the mission compound. It had never been so lively at morning services. At the prompting of Pastor Elijah, Joshua moved up to the altar and walked Ganeh back to his seat, before the singing of the closing hymn and the final prayer by Pastor Elijah. As the worshippers streamed out of the church, they spoke only of the incredible testimony given by Ganeh. Some of them were members of the Church's Ladies Round Table. They drew aside and discussed the revelations they were privileged to share with others at the service. Before they broke up, they decided that they would propose at the next Round Table meeting, the setting up of a fund to which donations would be made in cash or kind for Ganeh's rehabilitation.

In the temple, Joshua kept Ganeh in his seat, till the temple was empty of worshippers, before leading him through the vestry to meet Pastor Elijah. The pastor told Ganeh that he had been brave while giving a testimony that revealed so much of his failings. "You need changes in your life. Confession should be a start of that change. May God, give you the strength and courage to go on with it.," he said.

"This is my prayer," Ganeh replied.

"Amen.," the pastor said, resting his hand on his shoulder.

"When will you be seeing my Aunty Macile." Ganeh posed the question lamely as though he did not mean to ask it. He could not afford to pressure the pastor and lose his support.

"I shall be leaving soon to visit her. I have already sent her a note warning her that I shall be visiting her this morning with some of our elders. You will wait here at the mission. till we are back. We will then take things from there. Joshua will show you around," he told him.

Chapter 20

At 11.30 a.m., Pastor Elijah and six of the church's elders, walked out of the mission compound into Parsonage Street. They made their way to the junction of the street with Molu Road, then turned left into it. Thursday was a market day. The road was congested with traffic flowing into Munga from the provincial towns. Traders manning sidewalk stalls had already established themselves at the edge of the narrow footpath, leaving it narrower still. Pastor Elijah and his mediation group had to walk in single file for the first fifteen minutes of their journey, before entering the road section where the footpath was wider and traders fewer. A hundred metres on, was the entrance to Seley Road, where Aunt Macile's house was. It took the party another twenty minutes on Seley Road, before arriving there.

The house was a small sand-cement block building resting on large flat grounds with fruit trees in the back yard. There was a low timber fence and a gate at the front of the house. Aunt Macile was expecting them, so the gate was wide open when they arrived. Pastor Elijah led the way through the gate and knocked at the door. A young girl opened the door and let the party in. Aunt Macile was seating in a high chair by her window. She rose to welcome them and dismissed the girl.

"Pastor it is nice to see you. I was not at the morning service today. Is this visit intended to be a mission to deliver a reprimand?"

"No Sister, not at all."
"When I see the number accompanying you, I imagined the worst."
"Well, you may be right. It is a matter, which you might say, has some seriousness, but it is for your assistance that we are here."

Pastor Elijah began to lay out Ganeh's story, piece by piece and as delicately as he could, not mentioning his name. He said it was a young man in deep distress who needed comforting and reassuring of his confidence. Macile was looking straight at him as he spoke. It appeared as if she did not want to move her gaze away for even a second, in case she missed a word of what the pastor was saying. As soon as the pastor revealed that the young man was her estranged godson, she was overcome with joy. She could not contain herself in her seat. she stood and jumped in the air singing, "Hallelujah, My Godson is alive! God has done it. God had done it for us." The visitors joined in, holding hands and dancing around Macile. Pastor Elijah was pleased that he had been successful with the first part of the mission. He had to get Macile to help with bringing reconciliation between Ganeh and his parents. When calm had returned, Pastor Elijah said, "Macile, we rejoice with you and your family that God has brought Ganeh back to his own. My elders and I would like your assistance in getting him united with his parents."
"This will not be an easy matter. For my part, I will like to see him and give him every help he needs to get back to normal life, but for his parents, you should remember that they have lived with his loss for a long time. They

were told in a letter sent by a friend of his, that the mining work camp in which he was, suffered a deadly attack by rival miners and he was one of those killed. It described the horrible way his dead body was disposed of. It was also reported that the police had failed to solve the murder and had closed the case. I suggest that you call my sister Banie. She lives only two doors from me. She should be informed about this."

"We intend to call on her too. Ganeh told us you were her favourite aunt and was the one who would be readier to come to his aid. That is why we came here first. I have reserved the rest of the day to see this matter through. By the grace of God, I hope that with you, we will find a way to loosen his parents' hearts."

"If you wish, I will send my granddaughter over to inform her that you have been here and will be calling on her in a few minutes."

Aunty Banie was at the door when she heard the noise of footsteps on her gravel frontage.

"Enter good people," she said.

"Good day to this house," the visitors said in entering the front room of the house.

"Welcome! Can I offer you some akara? I have just finished making it."

"How can we turn down such generosity," Pastor Elijah said.

"This will hold out in the stomach till lunch time." She spoke as she handed around small portions of the delicacy on paper plates.

"Thank you so much. I haven't had these for some time."

"Be my guest." They ate silently, everyone waiting for someone to initiate another round of conversation. Pastor Elijah obliged.

"Banie, we haven't been seeing you and Macile at weekly morning services these days," he ventured.

"That's true. I have recently taken up giving private lessons to school children at the request of close friends. They are dissatisfied with the teaching of English and history to their children attending Munga Secondary. I still attend Sunday Morning Services and I am still active in the Women's Round Circle."

"The circle has been one of our most active church charities."

"We do our best pastor."

Banie rose to collect the plates. Two of the elders rose to help. "Please sit. Be at home. This is no trouble for me," she said, as she walked into the kitchen with the plates. On her return, Pastor Elijah gave the reason for their visit. He narrated everything about Ganeh, his unexpected arrival back from nowhere; how his mission was drawn to Ganeh and the cooperation he was seeking from her, to help his nephew become wanted and loved again by his family. He used the same calm and careful approach as he had applied earlier, in speaking to Macile. And it worked, but in a different way. Unlike Macile, she went pensive for a while, then said, "Pastor, this is unexpected news. The disappearance of Ganeh was like a bad dream, which has never left my mind. I must tell you, that I am confused right now. Perhaps, we ought to see his mother along with Macile. It will do us all good, sharing emotions over this inexplicable situation. I don't know whether, that can be done today. We ought to consult Macile about this. If she is up to it, I would be happy to go along with her to see Rose."

"I will arrange this Banie. God wants this done. I have given up all my engagements for the day to attend to this emergency."

The mediation party left Aunt Banie's house with the task they had set themselves, still far from being achieved. The pastor was trapped in a web of uncertainties from which he was desperate to escape. He decided to undertake the next step suggested by Banie without the elders. They may be needed later, he thought, but he saw the new situation as one which required only him from the mission. He addressed them as they walked up the road from Banie's house. There was anxiety in his voice.

"It will be best now for you to return to the mission, while I follow up Banie's suggestion."

"We think that is a good idea."

They walked away while he marched briskly behind them. When they looked back, he had disappeared into Macile's house.

Moving from one house to the other, he could reach agreement with the sisters for a visit to Rose, and if possible, one to Malu, his brother, before it was dark. Accepting the urgency which the pastor had put on his mission, it was agreed that the three should make these visits as soon as the ladies could get themselves prepared.

Within twenty minutes of their decision, they were making the journey to Wilmot Street where Rose and Madika lived. When they reached the Munga Anglican Church at the top of the street, it was then that they realized that Rose had not been given any notice of their visit.

"Rose will be livid seeing us turning up at her house without warning," Banie warned.

"We are not that heartless Banie to throw a mother this kind of information like we were feeding a chick in a pen," Macile remarked.

"I think it will be best if you both leave the talking to me," the pastor said. "I shall introduce the matter as calmly and as compassionately as my training demands."

"Alright pastor, but as relatives, we shall have a say in Ganeh's welcome into our family, if you don't mind. Rose has not always been open with us about happenings on her side of the family. Even with Ganeh's disappearance from home, it was only after we had heard the news from a neighbour of theirs, that she and that dumb brother of ours managed to sum up courage to tell the rest of the family about it. And he had the effrontery to ask for our help in tracing him, shedding crocodile tears." Macile was agitated as she spoke.

"That's over now Macile. Let's get on with what we have to do," Banie tried to calm her sister, speaking slowly and with some tenderness.

The pastor was ahead of the sisters when they reached Rose's house. He wanted Rose to see a friendly face first, when she opened the door. But it was an old man that showed up.

"Come in Pastor," he said, recognizing him.

"Is Sister Rose in?"

"She is on the back porch. I shall let her know you are here. Please sit, she will be with you soon."

He ushered them to three seats, then went off through a door opposite to where he has placed them.

Whatever strategy the pastor had planned to employ to ease Rose into accepting the news that Ganeh was alive, evaporated as soon as Rose came through the door. Seeing Banie and Macile before her with the pastor seating between them, she exploded into a frenzy. She fell to the floor, rolling, and kicking. She was crying and shouting, "Lord have mercy, Madika is dead! Don't put it any other way. Just tell me!" No one could console her, she was screaming persistently and so loud, that she heard nothing of Pastor Elijah's plea to stop and listen to him. Within ten minutes of the eruption, the house was inundated with neighbours, wanting to know what tragedy had befallen the house.

While the pastor was assuring the neighbours that Rose had reacted badly to their surprise visit, Macile in desperation, knelt and raised her up.

"What is wrong with you Rose?" she said. Then taking her into her arms, she shouted,

"Your husband is not dead, and so is your son Ganeh. He is back and in the care of Pastor Elijah. Can't you believe that? You should rejoice not shed those unwarranted tears." The words hit Rose like a lightning bolt. She became blinded by the tears gushing out of her eyes. She held firmly to Macile, trembling uncontrollably.

"It is not my son," she cried. "It is his ghost. Ganeh is dead. Miners killed him years ago. We had confirmation of his death from his friend. He described the attack on his work camp, the way he died and how his dead body was disposed of. The police failed to solve the murder. They closed the case, not caring whether or not he had relatives."

"We know how painful that news was, but there is hope now that there had been a mistake," Macile said.

"The grief is still raw, please don't rub in your spiteful salt. We have mourned his death every day for nineteen years."

Macile's patience was exhausted.

"Banie, you go talk to her," she said. Banie took Rose by the shoulder. She took her away from the curious crowd of concerned neighbours to a corner of the room where no one could hear them, and said to her,

"Pastor Elijah has seen him. He is taking care of him at his mission."

Drying her eyes and putting her dishevelled dress and hair in place, Rose said,

"He doesn't know Ganeh. Anyone can impersonate him. These days, crooks try every trick they can find to distress the unsuspecting,"

"I believe that it may not be so in this case."

Rose then pushed Banie to one side, as if parting a curtain "OK, let us go," she said defiantly, walking back to the crowded section of the room. When she reached where Macile and Pastor Elijah were standing, she said with a loud voice, "Let's go and see this man calling himself Ganeh." Without changing her dress, she grabbed the head tie covering her work basket of floral beads and walked out of the house. Banie followed her. She took her hand, fearing that she might trip and fall on the gravel road. The other two, walked behind them.

The mission compound was quiet when Pastor Elijah, Rose and her sisters-in-law arrived. The 12:00-noon service had ended and worshippers had dispersed. The four were expected, so they were ushered into the chapel annex. Each had their minds focussed on disparate objectives. In Rose's case, it was to prove the pastor wrong. Her fury at incorrectly concluding from the unexpected presence of her sisters-in-law, that Madika had died, had not subsided. She felt disturbed that the possibility that it had happened should have crossed her mind. As soon as they entered the temple, the pastor excused himself and walked out, his quick steps reminiscent of his days as a hospital orderly at Pennson Hospital. When he returned, he was heading a procession of elders to the altar. This was a formality drilled into church officers. No ceremony was to be demeaned which required the guidance and blessing of the Most High God. Even the induction into office of newly appointed administrative staff, required a ceremony at this temple with all protocols observed, including the formal entry into the chapel.

After a short prayer, the pastor invited Rose to the altar and had her stand beside him. He told her that he was going to have Ganeh brought in so she could confirm or not if he was her son, before they could deal with the matter of reconciliation and his acceptance into the family. There was no nervousness in her voice when she said, "I understand pastor." At a subtle nod of the pastor's head, one of the elders left the temple. Five minutes later she walked in with Ganeh, holding him by the hand, like a candidate for anointing. When they were half way down the aisle, the pastor walked towards them with Rose following. When she was able to make out the features of her son, she ran towards him, screaming. He quickly freed himself from the grip of his escort and waited till his mother reached him.

Banie and Macile watched the two as they embraced. It was a moving moment for all who watched the scene, many with lumps in their throats. Banie and Macile feared that Rose might suffer a terrible seizure, so they rushed to meet them. Within minutes, every one of the elders in the room moved to encircle them, clapping, and singing in praise of God.

Pastor Elijah then moved up to the altar with mother and son. Ganeh then spoke, recalling his experiences, and making a plea for forgiveness. His words floated across the temple like a discordant sound, little of it made sense to Rose. She seemed to be in a daze. Her heart was full of joy, but her body trembled from the shock. The sisters then went up to the altar, and brought her back to settle down in a seat between them. Soon the sisters became embroiled in heated exchanges. Observing this, Pastor Elijah dismissed the assembly with a prayer. He then invited the sisters and Rose to his study and appealed to them to take a constructive role in healing the wounds of the past, and work with him to get Ganeh united with the whole family.

Chapter 21

Malu felt relaxed and refreshed the morning after his night of rowing with Cecala. The tension and frustration of the evening had eased. He had come out of the verbal encounter with her, a new man. He had saved his marriage. Losing the job he craved was shattering; his local image damaged. But to suffer another blow, if their disagreement had led to a breakup, would have destroyed him. He could not have survived it. He had no lectures to give that day till 2.30p.m., then a seminar to attend at 5.00. He left home early that morning to reach the hospital at 8.30, the time he was told his father would be transferred to a general ward. On a normal day, he would still be in his study, preparing to leave for the institute, after an early breakfast with his kids, a meal Cecala insisted should be at 7.30. That left her time to get the kids ready for school.

His day's commitment at the institute was his least concern as he drove down the hills into the coastal fringe where Pennson hospital is located. It was windy when he left home, although the sun shone mildly, giving hopes of brighter sunshine later in the day. April misleads as it often does. Even in bright sunshine, light rain could descend at short notice from the thin clouds above. True to its nature, the April many love for organizing weddings, showed its watery face that Thursday morning. By the time Malu reached the hospital, and parked his car, it was raining heavily. Without any rain gear, he had to rush through the main gates to the enquiries desk, fully exposed to the weather. He had been told by his friend Radel, that his dad would probably be transferred to Ward 6, the male cardiology ward. He gave this information to the officer at the desk, who made the necessary consultations and then sent him off with an orderly to the ward. Taking out a handkerchief from his pocket, he dried his hair and face, as best he could. He had always boasted of having the knack of preparing to deal with unexpected situations when they arose. Not being prepared for the weather that day angered him. When he reached the ward, he had to endure the further embarrassment of being told by the nursing sister in the ward, that his father's transfer had been delayed for an hour because of the rain. "Sorry Professor Koney," she said. "We are not expecting the transfer of your dad to take place till the rain ceases. The walkway to the men's cardiology ward is uncovered. We might be able to do it in an hour or so. Unfortunately, you are not allowed in the Intensive Care Unit once a transfer has been authorized. Don't worry these April showers don't last that long," Malu was surprised that the sister knew his name, but tried not to show it. He merely said, "Thanks. That gives me time to dry up. I'll be back."

He called his wife and informed her, that the transfer of his father to a general ward had been postponed because of the sudden downpour. He said that besides the delay, he was caught in the rain and , was drenched.
"Go over to Mum's and wait till the transfer is done," she said. You can dry out there and borrow an umbrella before going back to the hospital.

"That's a good idea," Malu answered. He said it, but did not mean it.

"It was a bad idea," he thought. Looking miserable and stupid in front of his mother-in-law was not his idea of a solution for his predicament. Malu, the epitome of sophistication and decorum should put himself in a position that would belittle him in the eyes of his in-laws? Not him. He would rather lie again to save his face, than be the subject of gossip among Cecala's legions.

He thought of a better idea. He got out of the hospital and walked to the nearest market. It was only five minutes from the hospital. It is the oldest market in the city. It sold everything from apparel and household goods at road level, and food items at the lower levels and on its wide water front. He walked into a small clothes store and came out with a change of clothes, an umbrella and a plastic bag containing his wet clothes and shoes. He walked to his car, dumped the bag in and went back into the hospital. On entering Ward 6, he walked up to the Nursing Sister. As soon as he reached her desk, the sister rose to greet him.

Malu had only one thought in his mind as he faced the sister in charge. It came out muffled in his breath. "What else has she up her sleeves this time?" She smiled at him, saying, "I see Professor Koney that you managed to get a change of clothing already. You came in soaking wet this morning," she said.

"Yes. Thanks to the shop keepers not far from your doorstep," he replied

"It won't be long now. The orderlies have left to bring Mr. Koney over from the ICU."

"How strange; you seem to know my name, while I have no name to match your face."

"I am Nursing Sister Bidar. My son is a biology student at Horton Institute. He admires you a lot."

"But I do not teach any science courses. I teach African and Contemporary history."

"He is a member of Waitman Hall. He tells me you are the Master of the hall. The students there hold you in high esteem."

"I am flattered, sister. In truth, I should be receiving the students' dislike for my firmness in insisting that the Hall Warden enforces compliance with hall regulations and be stricter in maintaining discipline in the hall. Away from home, some students can be very unruly."

"The ways of the young are as baffling to them as to us their parents."

"We cannot avoid dealing with the exigencies of our time, sister. The pressing danger is the radicalization of the young."

"Here Professor, the orderlies are here. Can you please wait a few minutes in the corridor, while we rig him up and settle him in bed?"

"Surely sister." He walked past the medical team wheeling his father into the ward.

Ten minutes later, Sister Bidar called him back into the ward and escorted him to his father's bedside. He stood uneasily looking past the bed unto the folds of the curtain which the nurse had drawn across his space to afford them some privacy. His father looked up and smiled. He was a little frail, and was connected to a tube delivering medication through a vein in his right arm.

"Are you all right son?" He spoke with a concerned voice.

"I am. Good morning, it's just that I wonder how we got to this point with your health. When you leave hospital, Radel is going to keep a closer eye on you than before."

"How much longer do the doctors say I have to stay here?"

"You've just been brought in here. You seem to be making good progress. I am relieved about that, so don't worry about discharge just yet. The doctors will determine that."

They talked for another thirty minutes, about the family, and the action he had taken to get word to some of the family that he was ill.

"Why do you have to strain yourself tracing family? I will be out soon."

"At the critical time of your illness, Cecala and I felt that it was right to inform family, so they could use the opportunity to see you. We would not like to have it on our conscience that we kept your condition secret from the family."

"Is Cecala fine. You told me some time ago that she was battling to save her latest pregnancy."

"She is doing fine. We think she has got over the danger of losing it."

"That is good news. Your mother would be pleased too. She would like to have a lot of grandchildren."

"Mothers always do. She would have to be content with three. I don't see Cecala willing to go through another difficult pregnancy after this one. I have engagements at the institute this afternoon. I am sorry I will have to leave soon. I will be back tomorrow afternoon, God willing."

Before he left, he told his father that as he was getting better, he would bring his mother to see him.

Malu had two 50-minute lectures to deliver at 2.00 p.m. At the end of his lectures, he went straight to a seminar at 5.00 with his research students, whose research projects were based on the life and times of Mansa Musa, the tenth Mansa (King) of Mali. Students and lecturers carrying out research into other African empires and periods attended the seminar. The seminar took more than the 90 minutes allocated to it. A considerable interest was shown in the work presented by Datoh, one of Malu's students, whose research objective was to investigate the grounds on which Mansa Musa had claimed the throne of the Mali Empire. He referred to the writings of Arab scholars like *Ibn Khaldun* and *Ibn Battuta*, in which it was recorded that Mansa Musa had been the source of the story describing the manner of his succession to the office of Emperor, and so he suggested that Musa's claim was open to question. Musa's story was that Abubakari Keita II, the king he succeeded, had embarked on an expedition to explore the limits of the Atlantic, from which he did not return. Since he, had been appointed deputy to the king before he left on his fateful journey, he felt that it was his right to claim the throne.

Datoh found from searching the works of other reliable scholars, that it was the practice of kings going on pilgrimages to Mecca or some other mission, to appoint a deputy and later to name him his heir. Nevertheless, he intended in his paper to test the hypothesis that Musa's version of the method of his accession to the Malian throne, was from a man concealing the true account of the manner of that succession.

During discussions, which followed the student's presentation, Professor Sideko, Professor of Arabic Studies, disputed the student's submission, questioning some of the sources he had quoted. He argued that the student was following paths which great researchers had trod and had failed to find anything suspicious about Musa Keita's rise to power. Malu agreed that there were flaws in the student's argument, but advised that he examined, more writings of early African researchers. "There were outstanding revelations still to be prized out of these early writings, to negate your supposition that Musa's succession could have been improper," he said.
"True sir. But warlords operated widely in ancient Africa," he said.

He explained that he had looked at some of these writings already, in a preliminary testing of his hypothesis. He had found confirmation that Sundiata the first Mansa was responsible for unifying the small city-states in the area, into a prosperous empire, but he had accomplished this by using warlords. He made further defence of his line of thinking, emphasizing that he had not seen any evidence in his searches to suggest that warlords were forbidden to operate within the newly established empire. Such warlords might have been available to help ineligible aspirants usurp the throne. He said that it was known from early written records, that, a court slave, named Mansa Sakoura, who was freed by Sundiata Keita, and who had also served as a general, usurped the throne of Mali in 1285.

Besides, it was common practice, he said, for rulers in Africa and elsewhere to be succeeded by someone linked to them by direct blood lineage. The link of Musa Keita to Abubakari Keita II was suspect and his appointment as deputy was questionable. Furthermore, Musa appeared in many western reports as Kankou Musa and Kankan Musa, deepening the suspicion that he could claim lineage with Abubakari Keita II."

Many other comments were made on the student's approach to the study of the inheritance tradition among the kings of Mali. Malu then asked the student to revisit his examination of the lineage of the Mansas from the first Mansa to Abubakari Keita II, warning that there were many lineages established and broken throughout the history of the empire.

"We have from these same records you have quoted, that Mansa Musa was the grandson of Sundiata's half-brother. This makes your hypothesis more difficult to prove. You might find it difficult to save your hypothesis from attack, unless you could show that the empire of Abubakari did not enjoy social and political stability in all parts of the empire during Abubakari's reign," Malu said. The seminar was dragging on beyond the ninety minutes allocated. He closed the session, announcing that there would be another, the following week.

Malu reached home to find the sitting room of his house taken over by a crowd of people, most of whom he could not recognize from the door way. He could see his mother, Aunt Macile and Aunty Banie clearly, because they sat facing the open door. How the family got around to choosing those different titles which connote the same meaning for those two, remained a puzzle. Malu had known from childhood that you addressed these aunts in that way. His knees wobbled as he stepped nearer the assembly of guests. All eyes turned towards him. He took the next few steps like one walking into a fiery furnace. He could feel the heat closing in on him as if emanating from those steady eyes. He dropped his briefcase as Cecala left the visitors to welcome him. Her soft hug and a peck on both cheeks were unusually weak. He imagined trouble ahead, but stilled his nerves for it. He forced himself to read from her eyes, the purpose of the unexpected descent of such a mixed bunch of visitors, and learnt nothing until Cecala obliged.

"Your family and some people from Munga are here," she said.

"What did they say is their mission? I have already planned to see my aunts in the morning to brief them about the improvement in Papa's condition and let them know that he could now receive visitors during normal visiting times."

"Well, they are here now and with a pleasant surprise for you."

They walked slowly to join the visitors. The heat of anticipation of a miserable confrontation with his aunts intensified as he examined in his mind, every issue relating to his family that could trigger a toxic debate with the group. All he could think of was the terrifying confrontation his aunts had with his mother on the night of his father's sudden heart attack. His mother had told him that they had been verbally abusive towards her, and insensitive to the state of anxiety in which she was at that sorrowful moment. He was certain that Cecala had knowledge of the impending row, which she subtly avoided to disclose. Malu walked over to greet his aunts. He was stretching his hand to meet Aunty Banie's when a tall slim somewhat old man rose from his seat and ran to meet him. He embraced him and tried to speak. Startled by this sudden embrace from a man he didn't recognize he tried to release himself from his grip. The man held on and stood locked in embrace for nearly five minutes speaking inaudibly amid unrestrained weeping. Malu could only make out the words, "My little brother. Brother, I am your lost brother, Ganeh." He threw his hands around him and both held on as if nothing could separate them. "Welcome dear brother. What joyous moment this is. You have come at a time when Papa is still unwell. Sadness overwhelms us but you have brought happiness to lighten its impact," he said.

He was expecting something different, a family upheaval, at best. Instead he was experiencing a family re-union. His mother was seated sandwiched between his aunts with heads bowed, their arms around her trying to control the eruption of emotion that overcame her, seeing her two sons locked in filial embrace. It took her mind back to the years she pined for her eldest son's return.

When the two brothers released their grip on each other, Malu took his elder brother's hand and escorted him back to the chair he had occupied before their emotional reunion. He walked back from settling Ganeh into his seat and went around the room welcoming each of the visitors with a handshake and a word of gratitude for their presence. When he reached his mother, he said, "Mama, I had planned to visit you this evening after dinner to give you an update on Dad's progress. What a happy reversal?" She was already sobbing, having been so moved by the spontaneous display of emotion between the two brothers. She could not shake his hands, only bent down, reached for a handkerchief in her handbag, and dried the tears dripping down her cheeks.

As soon as Malu had finished his round of greetings and had taken a seat, Macile promptly stood up and began to speak. No one had appointed her spokesperson for the occasion. It was Pastor Elijah, whom Banie and Rose had expected to continue with his role as guardian and mediator, since taking in Ganeh the night before. He had given up his time and other commitments to help Ganeh back to normal life with his family. He had done so much in such a short time.

Macile started by apologising to Cecala and Malu for the surprise visit to their home.

"Malu," she said, "This is a surprise for you, but from what I have observed, it is a pleasant one."

"Certainly, Aunt Macile, it is," Malu replied.

"We have come with Aunty Banie and Rose, your mother. With us, are our pastor and some members of our church."

She then made a quick introduction, starting with the church's head, Pastor Elijah. She then took some minutes going through family history, most of which Malu had not heard before. Aunty Macile described the home his brother and Rose had built in Munga, as a home of love. She said that the couple had very little to boast of except the children God gave them. She explained how that home had been deprived of happiness, since the loss of their two eldest children. She said that one had been found and she gave praise to the Lord for His goodness.

Macile could not resist being her contentious self, so she complained that over the years, she and her sister had been kept ignorant of problems in their lives, some of which they were able to solve. To Banie's horror, she moved on to criticize Rose for isolating him from them, his closest living family, claiming that even as she spoke, she and her sister had not been given up to date information about their brother's condition in hospital. Rose was uncomfortable listening to Macile's diatribe. She turned to look at her with a scowl. "Don't talk," Banie advised, holding her down. Her practised firmness as a teacher, forestalled a clash that could have damaged the healing process that was in progress. After rambling on for another fifteen minutes, she finally arrived at the real purpose of their visit.

She recounted the events of the day pointing out that with their cooperation they had persuaded Rose to go with them to see Ganeh at Okeju Church mission where he had taken refuge.

"It was painful to hear Ganeh disclose to us the life he had lived during the thirty or more years of his self-imposed isolation from his family and his shameful admission of failure, she said."

While she spoke, Ganeh's eyes wandered around the room, taking in the fine furniture and artefacts on the walls. His brother had done well for himself, he thought. He had experienced sympathy from unexpected quarters over the last few hours and was feeling entitled to more. His face lit up when his aunt turned to him, as she said, "I have never before seen such display of emotion between mother and child."

After Macile's long speech, Banie saw her opportunity to get a word in.

"I am happy that we have been able to cover so much ground in a single day. Every emergency needs rapid action," she said. "It is so much appreciated, Aunty Banie," Malu commented.

"The appreciation goes to you, pastor and your elders, in double measure."

"I gave this day to this task. Now I must leave the family to take over what I pray will be a great and joyful duty."

He walked out of the house with his elders. The family were left to pursue the final leg of Ganeh's walk back into the family fold.

Chapter 22

The morning after the meeting at their house to introduce Ganeh, Malu and Cecala discussed what part they could play in Ganeh's re-integration into the family and the society. They were sitting at the dining table opposite each other. Malu had no lectures that day and Cecala was already back from dropping the children off at school and the nursery. They praised Pastor Elijah's efforts and the role Madika's sisters played in getting Rose to meet Ganeh.

"But why is Aunt Macile always so aggressive to your mum? She clashes with her whenever they meet," Cecala commented.

"She feels that her brother had married outside their ethnic group and continues to adhere to practices which their people had long since expunged from their culture," Malu said.

"It was with the same fowardness that she suggested that Ganeh should leave the mission last night and move in with Rose."

"Actually, I didn't see any problem with that."

Cecala wanted to say "how odd". She said instead, "Madika should have been consulted on the matter."

"What do we do now? He has moved out of the mission now. We cannot just send him back there. Pastor Elijah has handed our problem back to us."

"Then let's have him here until Madika accepts him again as his son. That would be a great brotherly gesture."

"Just hear that." His mind was examining the proposition. "You didn't want a maid to reside in the house permanently to help out with the kids. Even when you were so ill and had to be confined to bed for most of the time, you did not want any uncensored language or unruly behaviour from any   maid to be copied by your children."

He ignored her.

"Let's see if we can sort this out with Dad," he said.

"Approaching your dad will not be easy. You heard from Macile, how difficult it was for mum to be convinced that the report of Ganeh's reappearance was genuine. Just imagine how much more traumatic it would be for Madika? These things should be done carefully and by persons skilled in communicating news that have the potential to shock the recipient."

"I know. He may surprise us. He will be pleased to see Geneh back in the house with Rose, now that he is away."

There was nothing else to say. Malu seemed reluctant to have his brother residing in the house. It was thoughtful and generous of Cecala to suggest that he should now live with them. Granted that he was happy that the enigma surrounding his brother had been cleared, yet, he had doubts about his psychological wellbeing. He had been away in the wild for so long, and that must have had some lasting effect on him. It was a risk he was unwilling to take. He would help in other ways to get him back on his feet, but not to be living with him and his new family.

They stayed silent for a while, each of their minds examining their positions on a contentious issue. Then Cecala asked, "Why don't you consider raising this issue with your aunts?"

"That may be a good idea, but they were the ones who insisted last night that Ganeh should leave the mission and go back to live with Rose."

"Look Malu, that was a decision taken at the height of euphoria, when you were all excited about his so called 'resurrection from the dead.'"

"True. However, dealing with this situation again when a collective decision had been taken, can rebound badly."

"Fair is fair. Your dad ought to be told what's going on behind him. First, he must be informed as gently as can be done, that Ganeh is back. I think this has to be done soon. You will need to bring in Pastor Elijah again before he hears the news from an outsider."

"That I agree. It is now known that Dad can now receive visitors other than immediate family members. I shall get in touch with the pastor later this afternoon and get Aunty Banie involved."

It was a nice day, bright skies and only a gentle breeze relieving the stuffiness he felt within the solid walls of the staff residence he occupied. He walked into the garden, his hands behind his back. He had so much in his mind, so many challenges weighing on him. He had to face them. He slowly paced the paved narrow path that ran between rows of potato vines, he and Cecala had planted just before the rains. He wondered whether the effort was worth it. They might not be there to harvest the tubers, when they mature. Two weeks earlier, he had received replies from universities overseas, to which he had written, enquiring about vacant positions in his field. There were two offers. One was North-Western University in the US. It was offering him a visiting professorship, in the absence of an existing vacancy. The quality of his academic record so impressed the authorities, that they proposed to pay him a stipend equivalent to a full professor's salary for one year, while he held the visiting position. During that year, the university expected an endowed chair to be vacant for which he could apply. With his credentials, he would easily be the favourite for the position, they assured him. He was not sure how risky it was to take this offer. After all he had recently been disappointed over the outcome of a race in which he was the favourite. One thing he had learnt from his recent let-down, was not to be certain of anything. The other offer was from Maiduguri University in Nigeria, which had an existing vacancy at professorial level. He was offered the position at twice his present salary. He had told Cecala about these offers, but had kept it secret from his friends until he had made up his mind about any of them. He wanted time to consider the offers seriously and wisely, before accepting any one of them. In time, he thought, all will be clearer to him.

He was back in the house after his garden walk. He went straight to his study and was about to start the review of a paper sent to him by a colleague, who wanted it published in the African Journal of Social Sciences, when Cecala burst into the room. "Radel is here to see you. He could not get you on the phone, so he came

himself. He has been getting repeatedly, 'The number you have dialled is busy' voice messages."
"The networks these days are so unreliable.
Did he say what the urgency was?"
"No. He wouldn't."
"It is unusual to come all this way if it wasn't serious. My hunch is that it may be about my dad."
"Just don't think it."
"I feel a strange feeling, although I hate to think the worst. Let's go see him."

Radel had been Malu's best friend since they were at Primary School. His parents were well off and lived in the opulent part of Munga. Their friendship was unique. Although each of them was welcomed in each of their parents' home and were treated as a son of theirs, their parents never met socially. The Koneys felt that the Lamaras were snobbish and spoke only English at home, even to their servants, who struggle to understand their instructions. There have been some disastrous consequences from that practice, which was leaked to the community although the family tried to suppress it. It had been different with Malu and Radel. Their generation had turned all that around. Each family shared with the other, every secret, every joy, every disappointment.

Malu was in the sitting room in a flash. He couldn't have reached there faster, if he was escaping from a fire in his study. Cecala was behind him when he reached Radel. Before his friend could say a word, he asked, "Radel, it is

1.30 in the afternoon. What's so urgent that takes you out of your clinic at this time of the day?"

"There was an incident at the hospital this morning which may have caused Dad some setback in his condition. Like me, the cardiologist, Dr. Boya couldn't reach you on the phone, so he called me."

"Sounds serious then."

"He says it is a situation he is dealing with. Let's give him a day or two to see how Dad responds to the procedure he has carried out."

"You are not saying much Radel. I am deeply concerned." Malu was getting impatient. He was anxious to know what kind of setback his friend was talking about. He turned to Cecala, who was equally disturbed by the tension Radel was putting them under. She feared that he was not telling all he knew. "This is it, Radel," she exploded. "You know us better than that. We can take the shock. Look. Out with it. We had one only yesterday with Ganeh just showing up after an age, when we thought he was dead. That did not destroy us."

"What Ganeh? Malu, you mean your long lost brother is back?"

"That is a long story. Let's leave that for another time," Malu said

"Alright then. To the scare at hand, there is no point in giving you medical details I do not know. He does not know yet what caused the relapse. He is surprised it happened and will be finding out the cause."

"Can we go to the hospital to learn more? We too are just as concerned. I was going to collect the children at two o'clock, but will ask Andrea my neighbour to do me the favour. We do help each other in that department."

Radel offered to drive Malu and Cecala to the hospital. He didn't want any of them to drive as they were obviously distraught not knowing how serious Madika's relapse was. He was doing this not merely out of loyalty to a friend, but because he felt responsible for ensuring that his patient had the best attention from the specialist consultant he had great professional respect for. He had personally chosen him among the other consultant cardiologists at Pennson hospital to handle Madika's case.

They travelled speechless: the only sound piercing the solid tenseness of the atmosphere that surrounded them was from the heavy beating of the car's engine. It was a ten-year-old Volkswagen Passat. He could afford better, but Radel was the kind of man who played down his wealth. This frugal attitude extended to other aspects of his life, except for his clinic. In that quarter, critics will find no cost spared to make it probably the most fashionable and the best equipped medical facility in the community.

Driving into the city from his friend's residence in the hills often thrilled Radel. He liked negotiating the sharp curves on the road, while taking in the majestic scenery spread out before him. That Friday, the drive was different for him. He was searching for answers to the sudden relapse which Madika had suffered, so it was a slow drive, one part of his mind concentrating on the road, the other struggling to find a possible cause for the sudden change in Madika's condition. He remembered the last time he was called to Madika's house when he suffered the stroke from which he was gradually recovering in hospital before this latest crisis. It was his second in three years. Radel had been managing his condition since his first attack, and was satisfied that his condition had been stabilized when that emergency call came. On that occasion, it was the result of negligence on his part for failing to take his prescribed medication regularly, combined with the shock news that Malu, the son who in his eyes had no match when it comes to brain power, was beaten in the contest for President of Kilinde Institute, that triggered it.

He had seen so many of these reverses in the course of his practice with timely surgery. He knows however, that this can be bad in the case of older patients with repeated heart attacks when subjected to excitable incidents or unexpected shock. Now there was nothing he could do but wait till he saw Dr. Boya to learn of the result of the procedure he had initiated. Nothing is more worrying than uncertainty, and it showed more in Malu and Cecala's faces. Their concern hung over their faces like a crumpled cloth. They could only hope that Madika would pull through, whatever the doctor's prognosis.

On their arrival at the hospital, Malu and Cecala were dropped off at the entrance while Radel found space to park his car. They found the reception hall cramped with emergency cases. The more serious ones had been brought in from an accident at Mamadori Hill, where a ten-ton truck had run into waiting passengers at a bus stop near the bottom of the hill. They had to force their way through this human barrier to reach the enquiries desk of the ICU. By the time Radel had parked his car and made a dash for the ICU, he met the couple already speaking to a duty nurse. Malu had been a regular visitor to the unit when Madika was first brought in. Some of the nurses knew him. They sometimes waived rules on visiting and length of visits, when he visited. Not this nurse. She would not allow them to see Madika. She was under strict instructions. No visitor should be allowed to see the patient. Dr. Boya was going to speak to the patient's private doctor who had referred him to his unit as soon as he could arrange a meeting with him. "I am Dr. Lamara, the patient's doctor." The words shot out came from the back of two heads tilting sideways to see the form of the man who might rescue them from humiliation. "He is expecting you. I'll let him know you are here. Please come with me to his waiting room." Malu and Cecala followed Radel as she escorted him out of the IUC reception hall. She walked briskly, the back of her nurse's cap clipped neatly on the Afro curls that stream on to the back of her neck. Her whole body spoke a language you understood if you had been a girl scout. "You will wait here," she said, and opened the door to the waiting room. Then like a top, she spun around and left.

The three entered the room, expecting to find no one else there. Then as the door sprung open, they gasped, as four figures came into focus. There seated before them, were Rose, Ganeh and her two aunts. Without warning of any kind, Macile rose and with outstretched arms, ran to embrace Malu crying, "Madika, Madika, Madika. Malu, my dear, our brother's condition has gone worse." Malu stood transfixed like a statue. He made no move to hold her. Radel, walked over to them. "We do not know yet how bad it is," he said. "I will see Dr. Boya soon to find out. He was in good spirits when we saw him this morning in the general ward," Macile said, struggling to speak between sobs. "Learning that he was well enough to receive visitors, we wanted him to see the reformed Ganeh, believing it might bring his father joy and lighten his spirit in this depressed environment."

"Don't be upset, he is in good hands," Radel assured her.

"Doctor, it happened before our very eyes. He was sitting upright at the edge of the bed when we came into the ward. We were with him for only a few minutes. Please help him."

Malu was kept trapped in the arms of her aunt as she spoke. Cecala sensing her husband's unease in that unpleasant embrace, moved to part him gently from the weeping Aunt Macile, and took her back to her seat. One glance at the still bowed heads, told her that between them they shared a guilt that was weighing heavily on their consciences.

The duty nurse came back from Dr. Boya to announce that the cardiologist would see Dr. Lamara in his office. There were no greetings, no pleasantries. "Take a seat Radel," he said. He was not full sunk into the padded armchair before him, when he said, "Doctor, your patient has had a massive rupture of the cardiac artery. We have carried out a procedure to attempt a bypass, but that was only partially successful. He is on life support right now. We intend to monitor his response throughout the night."

"Could any member of the family be allowed to see him? A whole lot of them are in your waiting room, anxiously waiting for information about him."

"They ought to be. They got the poor chap all worked up. That triggered the present damage"

There was anger in his voice now, as he went on to narrate what Sister Hassan reported in her notes, when the patient was brought urgently into his unit, all wired up with life-saving equipment

"If there is a sensible one among them who will not raise a riot at seeing him, I will permit that."

When Radel returned to the waiting room, everyone rose. They looked drained of everything, except the anxiety which shows on their faces, but more prominently on Rose's. He spared them the harsh words of rebuke that almost came out of his lips when he saw them. "Malu, please come with me." That was all he could say. On the corridor he told Malu everything he had learnt from Dr. Boya and prepared him to meet Dr. Boya. During the ten minutes with the consultant in which he was told of his father's state after his relapse, Malu was actually hearing nothing, until he felt the pressure on his arms when Radel took hold of him to lead him to the room where his father lay clinically dead, lines of pipes from his body to equipment flashing data on his vital organs, providing temporary life support. He tried to suppress the tears forming under his eyelids from flooding his eyes, but they kept building up till they started falling like rain drops off a tree leaf. He knew that there was nothing more the doctors could do for his father. It would be a question of time before his life support was switched off. There would be recriminations, a family row, blames, counter blames, regrets. Everything unreal or imagined would overshadow life in his family for years to come. He wanted to be as far away as possible from all of it. He would tell his wife that he would accept the offer from North Western University.

Another time, another place, let the brighter light shine.

REVIEWS

A PEN FOR A BRUSH

A Review

By

Oumar Farouk Sesay
Poet
Author of
The Edge of a Cry (poems) – SLWS, 2015
Landscape of Memories (novel) – SLWS, 2015
Broken Metaphor (poems) – SLWS, 2017

The story of love has been told many times and in different ways; the story of arranged marriages has also been told many times in varying ways; the story of societal attitudes towards the privileged and under privileged has been told many times over. Yet these recurring stories are retold in Koso-Thomas's novel, *A Future Imperfect*, with a vibrancy that makes them different and refreshing, begging the question, 'how did he do that?'

From the initial incident of a student strike at the university, the author anchors the story /stories of Malu and his dreams and aspiration against the backdrop of politics within academia. It reads like a linear narrative driven by cause and effect yet with a powerful undercurrent that takes everything in its path -- culture, politics and religion.

234

The story of Malu and Cecala revolves around love, work, ambitions, disappointment, violence and politics. The message lurking in every episode is that, to both elite or ordinary folk life is just one single script acted differently in different settings.

The author who is an Engineer by training, a poet and painter at heart, grabs pen lieu of a brush and paints a novel in lieu of a portrait. His description of traffic congestion in the city is so real the reader feels the torment of being stuck even on the pages. He renders activities and events like pictorial composition making the reader to ponder, is this fiction or fact or a cross between the two?

A Future Imperfect, is set in academia drawing characters from academics; it tells the stories of their imperfection, their humanities, and the resonance of their lives in the society beyond the idyllic environment of the campus. In this story, the author succeeds in pointing a search light in the darkness of a community's source of light. It is a laudable work that deserves to be read.

A Review

By

Eldred D. Jones
Emeritus Professor of English & Former Principal
Fourah Bay College
University of Sierra Leone

In *A Future Imperfect*, Koso-Thomas weaves a skillful narrative of a society still thrilled with the gadgets of a new civilization – new institutions of learning, modern hospitals, busy mines and Industries while still steeped in traditions heavy with beliefs seemingly pulling in an opposite direction. Underneath the glittering surface the human debris of broken lives, neglected populations unsupported by sophisticated social institutions rely on the services of Evangelists and prophets who sometimes stand in the way of modern science but occasionally pull off miracles.

The principal character Malu Koney stands at the cusp of international scholarship in African history but his sister has been lost in youth in the mysteries of traditional secret practices, while a brother had also disappeared having slipped off the narrow educational path into the unregulated underworld of the mining industry.

Manola, and the capital city Clendon, are set in scenes of spectacular beauty traversed by narrow roads one slip from which spells disaster. The accident in Clendon, in which a motorist hangs dangling precariously over a ravine from the branch of a tree, with a whaling crowd on the road watching him helplessly, almost moments to his doom, is a metaphor for the uncertainty of this life. The rescuing Fire Brigade arrives too late.

The novel opens with a dramatic demonstration of the society's own strength as a threat to its continued wellbeing. The university's students are in revolt. Its manicured lawns and beautiful gardens are thoughtlessly trampled over and stained with the very blood of its teachers. Yet it survives and the scene of scholarly democracy in which professors and research students debate the intricacies of the ancient empires of Mali, hold out an escape into sanity. Amid these contrasting forces, families with roots in deep history interact and grapple with the difficulties of modern everyday life – bringing up children, falling in love and getting on with life.

Malu and Cecale exemplify the mutual tenderness in which academic ambitions are fulfilled, and the shocks of disappointment are survived. Malu and his lifelong friend Radel, a doctor in the new crop of the science generation hold each other up through the trials of the new civilisation, while the crotchety aunt Macile is at the centre of family intrigue, which keeps alive the continuing conflict between the bright smooth mechanised future and the reluctant grumbling past.

Koso-Thomas weaves a skillful narrative through all the high ideals of university scholarship, of family life, of religious fervour and human suffering with exceptional skill and delicacy giving a rounded picture of a society, which is so easily misunderstood from a distance or cursory acquaintance.

A Review

By

Rhod A. Atere-Roberts
Swanley, Kent

This is an interesting narrative about the challenges of family life and work.

The juxtaposition of the politics of power can be decided rightly or wrongly with unexpected result that can be difficult to comprehend by ambitious individual.

Albeit though, the temptations which the individual faces in life, cannot be overlooked as, what he/she hoped for is not absolute.

Believing in oneself can prepare an individual mentally, morally, physically, and spiritually for the future ahead.

This is a well written novel and should be an interesting addition to the new stock of African novels.

A Review

By

Gloria Dillsworth
Retired Chief Libarian
Sierra Leone Library Board

For a full-length novel, Kosonike Koso-Thomas's *A Future Imperfect*, is masterly and fascinating. His prose is lucid and the main characters are vividly and interestingly portrayed.

Kosonike Koso-Thomas is artistic and creative and the novel is astonishing for it perception on the themes of University Politics, ethnic loyalties, ancestors, land disputes, local customs and traditions, in-laws, Pentecostal churches, and their Pastors.

These themes are well articulated and there are flashes of humour. The resulting book is an entertaining and gripping tale which keeps the reader engrossed and the attention fixed from beginning to end.

It is sometimes stated that novels by some African Writers are either "too African" to be appreciated by non-Africans or they are "not African enough"! Kosonike Koso-Thomas writes with great style and sensitivity. The themes in this novel are universal, and *A Future Imperfect* will capture the imagination of many readers around the world. It should be a welcome addition to the present-day canon of novels by African Writers.

www.ingramcontent.com/pod-product-compliance
Lightning Source LLC
Chambersburg PA
CBHW031320170626
46807CB00002B/498